THE WOODLAND SPRITE SERIES

BOOK ONE
TAKEN BY STORM

ILLUSTRATED BY NUNO GOMES VIEIRA

FLEUR ROSSDALE

To Riley and Kim Raybould

With love from Granny xx

CONTENTS

ACKNOWLEDGMENTS

Thanks to:

Robin & Louella Hanbury-Tenison; Merlin & Lizzie
Hanbury-Tenison; and The Castle Howard Estate
for providing key locations.

To:

The Wildlife Trust; The Woodmeadow Trust;
Dr Rupert Sheldrake; Dr Merlin Sheldrake;
George Robinson & Julia Raybould;
William & Rachel Robinson;
Susie & David Seligman; Edward & Catherine Rossdale
Julia Condon; Amanda Harling; Lupe Castro; and
Pascal d'Ursel
for information, encouragement and support.

Special thanks to
Antoine Laurent for his valuable mentoring,
Anna Berntson for her creative research and
Nuno Gomez Vieira for his illustrations.

To
The Northwood Fairy Trail, York,
for their architectural influence on fairy homes replicated in
the illustrations as manipulated photographs;
and St Nicks Nature Reserve & Environment Centre, York
for their Urban project strategies.

Much appreciation for her edit to
Lisa Davis

PROLOGUE

It all began one morning when it started to rain. By *it*, I mean a particular rainbow that led to my Eureka moment, which usually happens when a sprite catches a wish and everything becomes clear.

As the rain washed the woodland clean at the break of day, I watched other nature sprites living in and around Cabilla holding hands forming their rainbow across the sky. More in touch with the real world than traditional fairies, I marveled that the strength of their combined magic power could send wishes on the back of a shooting star up into the Universe, where wishes are picked up and granted.

Even without knowing that they were making a wish, I could clearly see that each one of them had a purpose of their own. Gazing at the remarkable arch, I realised that I had one too. I just had to find the true colour of my nature before I could join forces with other nature sprites in making rainbows.

At the back of my mind, I secretly thought that the Four Winds would help me in my mission, even though they had problems of their own.

I had not understood then that on top of it all, there would be so much more to gain.

And then, on that very same morning, the opportunity for the adventure arrived right on my doorstep, thanks to a robin redbreast named Robbie....

1

AN IMPORTANT ANNOUNCEMENT

Since the beginning of time, we sprites have developed powers of observation, sharpened our ears and adjusted a sense of smell to sniff out danger. But, perhaps, more importantly, our instincts help us understand the silent languages and magical truths hidden in nature.

So many wonderfully ordinary things happen from one day to the next that we often forget to notice them. For instance, before dawn, a hint of colour in the dark sky tells us that the sun is just about to peep up over the horizon.

This morning there is something more – I hear nature call on sprites to join the sun in the sky, and I know that this means rain. Sure enough, in the blink of an eye, nature sprites appear, heading towards rain clouds just as the sun comes up. Washed by the rain, they glow their own bright colours while holding hands and making a huge arch that stretches from one end of the landscape to the other and form a perfect rainbow.

The sudden downpour sends me flying out of my treehouse and onto my balcony to take a shower. Like other woodland sprites, I have to be ready to wash on the spur of the moment. Sea sprites living on our shores and the coastlines of the great continents are lucky enough to wash in the sea whenever they please, while snow sprites roll in the snow. But all other nature sprites, whatever the season, must wait for rain. As a result, I never take the weather for granted.

By the weather, I really mean the Four Winds. Every nature sprite is in awe of them, although we are equally afraid of their power because we rely on them for everything we need. In particular, they make the clouds that travel over oceans and lakes, absorbing moisture to bring rainwater onto the land, not only for us to wash, but so that everything can grow. So I welcome the rain as a wish come true, turning my face up to the sky with my eyes closed. I love to feel the splash of raindrops and the tickle of snowflakes against my cheeks.

Today, I enjoy the invigorating chill of autumn in the air. Showering outside with the rest of the woodland gives me a sense of friendship and unity. Leaves become glossy and shimmer. Branches sway with contentment. The rainwater has brought minerals to feed the soil, as it provides a nutritious drink of water to every living creature.

Peering over the top of my makeshift shower cubicle, I gaze longingly at the rainbow, an impressive balancing act on the part of my fellow fairy sprites. One day, I, too, will take my place in making rainbows and be blessed with the power of magic. But, for now, my little sister Anil and I will continue to glow with the white light of youth. We will just have to be patient until we shine the actual colour of our nature.

I finish my shower and sniff the sweet, musty smell of autumn in the air. I like the seasons equally for their differences. My little sister, Anil, loves springtime best, and I tease her that we're not meant to show favouritism. In fact, we are not allowed to favour one thing over another in the woodland. It doesn't matter if they're too small to see or as big as a badger: all living organisms are just as important as the next and could not exist without each other.

Flapping my wings dry, I watch the nature sprites of Cabilla fly back after the rain to protect rivers, wetlands, bogs and valley mires on the moors.

"Good morning, Sky," says a meadow sprite heading home, cartwheeling in the air and waving at me.

"What a lovely day," says another.

I throw out kisses that swirl around, blown by the breeze up and over and about, and watch the colourful sprites dart here and there to catch them as they head off towards home. Enjoying the happy feeling they have left behind, I smooth walnut oil over my delicate wings with the back of my hands to protect them from the harmful rays of the sun. Like human fingerprints, the criss-cross patterns on our wings are unique, reminding me that I am not the same as any other sprite.

I finish drying myself and listen to birdsong waft in

through my bedroom window welcoming the new day.

Birds stop to rest in my tree after long journeys to enjoy views over the river and meadows beyond. This means that I'm often one of the first woodland sprites to hear the news delivered by migratory birds as they arrive from faraway places. Some come from Scandinavia in the north, and others return from the warmth of Africa in the south, depending upon the season. I can't imagine flying all that way – I have never flown further than a few miles north.

Once the dawn chorus has died down, Robbie, a robin redbreast, flies up to land on the bird box on the tree beside me and sings a solo. He starts by making tut-tut trills to beckon those of us in earshot to gather around and listen. His thrilling, trilling tone is uplifting, and I'm pleasantly surprised to pick up the sweet smell of adventure in the crisp morning air.

Slipping into my slippers, I pull on my woollen dressing gown and tie it at the back like an overall with a bow under my wings. I head outside to listen to Robbie and sit dangling my legs over the edge of my balcony.

"I have important news," he announces. "Fairy folk are invited to pay their respects to the Four Winds at their temple," he sings at the top of his voice. "The ceremony will take place at a Nature Summit – as important as it is tall – in ten days' time. Sprites protecting the natural world are invited to apply for places and to host conservation warrior sprites at the Temple of the Four Winds at Castle Howard in Yorkshire." He pauses to take a breath. "The gathering kicks off with a service in the temple to give thanks. Afterwards, you are invited to attend the wedding of a pair of barn owls, where fairy folk, nature sprites and nocturnal animals will mingle and meet at a candlelit feast prepared by famous food fairies.

"Overnight guests, speakers and spectators will gather at the temple the next morning to share their nature stories. So far, I can confirm that desert sand sprites will bring news of the weather in the Middle East, and ice and snow sprites from the North Pole. With limited places, those wishing to apply must do so without delay."

I can hardly believe my ears but my excitement immediately turns to worry at the thought that Anil and I won't be able to go. Sprites have huge respect for the Four

Winds blowing from the north, south, east and west and everywhere in between, and I am no exception. Everyone, and that means *everyone*, will want to go.

As soon as Robbie has finished his song, I flutter my wings. It's like clapping, but the soundless delicate movement shows respect as well as enthusiasm and appreciation.

"Ecstatic," I say. "What a momentous event! Thank you for bringing this wonderful opportunity to us in Cabilla. How I would love to go."

"I've been spreading the news far and wide," says Robbie with a sense of pride. "From the Scottish islands of the Outer Hebrides and will not stop until I reach Lizard Point and Mousehole further south, but I can't take all the credit," he chirps. "Swallows and nightingales have taken the invitation as far as Africa where they will winter. Starlings, chaffinches and lapwings have dispatched invitations around Eastern Europe before arriving to spend their winter here."

"Amazing," I say. "But, it's sure to be packed, and we won't have a chance of going. Anyhow, Anil and I have never left Cabilla before."

"In that case," replies Robbie, bobbing his head and hopping on one leg. "That's all the more reason why you and your younger sister should go."

"I'd give anything to be there," I say. "But I doubt that we'll be allowed to leave the woodland as we're still only fledgling sprites."

"You'd be surprised, Sky," Robbie says, getting a little closer. "Lawmakers are sitting up and listening to the voice of the young. Stories brought by nature sprites living all around the world will push them to fight for change and make sure fledglings can enjoy a better world. You'd have your say."

My mind wanders, wondering what I might contribute if I am allowed to go. Looking out across the river, I hear the whisper of the breeze combing the grassy meadow and smell the damp sweetness it carries through the air. It's where I love to fly, playing with bees, butterflies and dragonflies in the summer. A few weeks ago, I collected an armful of wildflowers growing among the long grasses and hung them upside down in my kitchen to dry.

It was a windy day, and the swaying spikes of grass gently tickled my bare feet as I hovered above them. It made me giggle with enjoyment. I was pleased to gather vibrant blue cornflowers, wild purple orchids and a few ox-eye daisies. I made a flower arrangement and used some of the cornflowers to make a beautiful headdress. It would be perfect to wear in the evening at the Temple of the Four Winds.

"The peace and harmony found in nature must be preserved," I say wistfully.

"Absolutely," Robbie replies in earnest. "On my way down from Scotland, I passed a newly demolished woodland in the Midlands, destroyed to make way for a new train line when there's already a perfectly good one that could be mended instead. Angry animals and insects have set off on their long journey to camp out in Ray Wood beside the temple, to have their voices heard in protest."

"Animals are displaced all the time," I say, equally upset. "Making way for new roads and shopping centres that destroy their natural habitats. It must have been very distressing for you to witness."

"It was terrible," he answers mournfully. "Bulldozers flattened the ground to a pulp of mud, killing trees and hauling them up by their roots. And that's not all. I stood by and watched ploughs destroy meadows filled with insects and wildflowers. I felt helpless and ashamed."

Imagining Robbie's ordeal, I watch colourful autumn leaves blow gracefully, wafting here, there and everywhere. Ash and sycamore seeds shaped like helicopter wings spiral and spin, taken by the wind to land away from their parent tree.

"I wish there was something I could do to help the animals."

"You can. All you have to do is to turn up," he cheeps, "and speak up for them. So many will have nowhere to go and will not be welcome on other animal territories and need help. Become the voice for the voiceless."

"Will you be there?" I ask, unsure of what I would be able to do to find them new homes.

"For sure. I've volunteered as a reporter," he says, puffing out his chest feathers.

"Legitimate," I reply – it's sprite speak for something genuine and worthy.

"Top-notch conservation warrior sprites will be there," he says, taking a sip of rainwater collected in the bellflowers on my windowsill. "And Titania, Queen of the fairies, will preside over it all."

"Awesome! But, I'd clam up and turn shy meeting such remarkable conservation warriors," I say. "I'd feel hopeless compared to them."

"Believe in yourself, Sky. You never know, you might bring fresh new ideas," he says chirpily.

"I'd give anything to meet nature sprites from around the world and hear their stories first-hand."

Robbie flies off to a lower branch, where Anil lives. I watch him splash his feathers in the birdbath she keeps on her balcony for guests to use and make a wish.

"That's better," he cheeps enjoying a long drink. "It's good that the weather is set to be fine today,"

"Don't be so sure. It can be unpredictable these days," I reply.

2

AT HOME AND SCHOOL

Anil is not only my little sister, she's also my best friend. We do almost everything together. My treehouse is high up in the branches of a silver birch tree on the edge of Cabilla Wood and is connected to Anil's by a simple rope ladder. I love living so close to her – plus, climbing up and down the rungs is a lot of fun.

Although sprites usually live alone, we are social fairies. We like to invite guests over for lunch or tea. When we do, we go to great lengths to tidy up our homes, place flowers in vases, make jellies and bake our favourite cakes and pies. I love fresh, juicy brambles best. Of course, Anil is welcome to drop in at any time, and luckily the same goes for me at hers.

I splash my face with fresh raindrops collected in the bellflower cup. I am eager to discuss the invitation brought by Robbie with Anil and to ask whether she also detected a smell of adventure in the air. I quickly pull on a pair of woolly tights and a warm sweater, button up my favourite red leaf pinafore and climb down the rope ladder.

I find Anil in her kitchen, making a pot of mint tea.

"An adventure?" says Anil, laying a breakfast tray for two to take outside. "And raise our hopes about going to the Temple of the Four Winds, you mean?" she chuckles. "Let me see…"

Anil and I have an excellent understanding of the wind and are fluent in the language of raindrops. We can interpret their patterns on the ground and understand the meaning of cloud shapes and colours. Anil sniffs the air and frowns, listening attentively, attempting to pick up messages from sounds made by the wind rustling through the trees.

"Humph," she says, shaking her head. "There's something afoot, but it smells charred with danger." Anil stops dead, midway towards her balcony. "Yes, definitely something to do with burning," she adds, turning towards me with raised eyebrows. "Now I come to think about it, a gentle breeze awoke me in the middle of the night. It flicked my curtains, whispering something so softly that I couldn't quite make out what it meant as I was half asleep."

"Hmmm. Perhaps it was a personal invitation to their temple?"

"Dream on," she replies as I follow her out onto the balcony, wondering what it was the wind had wanted to tell her.

* * *

Our classrooms are dotted among the trees in the centre of the wood: a gym, a library, a lecture room, dining room, guesthouses for visitors and a place for meetings. Teachers fly in from far and wide to instruct us on new subjects and to open our minds to different points of view. They all teach essential values, especially being kind and telling the truth. We call this ruthful – the opposite of ruthless.

Anil and I are the only two apprentice woodland sprites living in Cabilla. Nevertheless, we meet many other nature sprites our own age when they join us for lessons in the woodland on selective subjects. Apart from attending classes, our daily job is to survey nature. This means that we observe trees, bees, birds, insects and animals to check that they are in balance with the rhythms of the sun, the moon and the four seasons. We also search for unpredictable behaviour or signs of sickness while making notes, jottings and sketches in our nature notebooks.

Our teachers are also sprites. They look after the welfare of woodlands and write books about the magic of nature. They live in treehouses in the centre of our woodland near the classrooms where we attend our lessons. We call them the Three Ws, which is short for Woodland Welfare Workers.

Straight after breakfast, Anil and I go to ask the Three Ws if they will allow us to represent Cabilla at the Temple of the Four Winds. They hum and haw between them and leave for quite a while to talk among themselves.

"You'll need to show us your knowledge of the hidden mysteries in nature that you particularly wish to protect," says Mr Woodward, our head teacher.

I am rather taken aback when Anil angrily answers him back and says it is unfair to even think about protecting one thing over another. I know she is right. This goes against everything they teach; they are constantly drumming it into us that we must never show favouritism over any aspect of our ecosystems. I worry that Anil will be in trouble and might have dashed our chances of going on the trip. But to my amazement, it seems to have impressed the Three Ws. It prompts Mr Woodward to ask why we are so keen to leave our beloved Cabilla to go on a trip away from home.

"We'd like to help displaced animals and meet other sprites and hear how they live compared to the way we do," I reply.

"Anything else?" he asks, peering over his glasses.

"And, of course, to help the Four Winds keep calm."

"Yes, yes, absolutely," says Mr Woodward. "It's vital that you young ones keep up the good work fighting for clean air, water, healthy soil and so on. It's the only way of protecting our natural world."

"We can think of nothing else apart from going to

the Nature Summit," says Anil tilting her head to one side.

In the end, the Three Ws agreed that we can go if we pass a written test.

We immediately begin revising and frantically looking things up in the library. Even though the chances of going are low, I cling to a glimmer of hope and can't help thinking about what I'll wear and will need to pack.

I stare into the woodland, daydreaming. I'm often told off for doing this, but it helps me unravel problems and see things more clearly. Rays of sunshine dart playfully through the trees, illuminating zillions of tiny fungal spores floating through the air, looking for a suitable spot to settle. I move a little closer and try to pick up their thought waves. I fail and decide to try again later.

I have a feeling that we might be asked about these magical spores in our test. Once they find a place to grow, they sprout shoots in every direction making a mass of threads. These connect with other fungi to form the Wood Wide Web, a root system that is just like a vast computer brain. I will try to work something about them into an essay, as they are vital to life on Earth. This network is also used for trees to send warning signals to neighbouring trees and pass chemical messages into the air when they are threatened. Anil is determined to learn their secret language. Everything is hidden in the magic of nature, she says, just waiting to be discovered.

A little mouse distracts me. It is squeaking in distress with something stuck in its throat. I fly down while wracking my brain for ideas to make it sneeze, as that's the only way I can think of dislodging whatever is causing the problem. Remembering the spores, I frantically look around for toadstools or mushrooms. As I had hoped, I see a troop of them, puff balls releasing spores, tiny dots swirling like smoke signals. These can bring on a series of sneezes and coughs in the same way as pollen. I encourage the little mouse to move towards the cluster and ask her to inhale. After a few deep sniffs, the mouse sneezes and sneezes and finally coughs – out shoots something very strange and pure white. I pick it up. It is small, hard and as flat as a coin, ridged at the rim. Whatever it is, it certainly does not belong in the woods. I will take it to show the Three Ws.

"That's better," she says. "Thank you, Sky. What a

fright I had." And off she scurries to get on with her day.

It isn't always quite so easy. Foxes and badgers battle each other over territory or compete for a mate and can cause serious injuries to each other. Hedgehogs are solitary creatures and only squabble among themselves over minor annoyances, probably because they have few defenses apart from their spikes.

When an animal is wounded in a fight or is very sick, or a tree is dying, and there's nothing I can do to make them better, I try to understand that this is part of the cycle of life. Dead animals and fallen trees are eaten, digested and deposited as nutrients back into the soil, helping new life to grow. This natural process maintains recycling systems without sentiment or waste. Instead of feeling sad when they die, they live on in my memory.

I look again at the object the little mouse coughed out. I don't recognise the material, so it must not be made of anything from our woods. But even worse, it could have choked her to death.

3

THE THREE WS

In class we study the colours of the rainbow, which Mr Woodward tells us combines every colour under the sun. There are over a million of them in these magnificent arcs, but only seven – violet, indigo, blue, green, yellow, orange and red – are easily seen by human eyes. A hundred colours that are tricky to detect are shown on a chart hanging on our classroom wall to learn.

Sometimes, I'm sure that my glow will end up being the poppy-red of determination, but other times, the dusky blue of calm seems to suit me better. It takes time for us to find out what we're really like. We cannot shine with our own tone until it is clear which one suits us best and, I am realising, is not something we can hurry.

Mr Woodward shines with the honey yellow of happiness and hope. His subject is wildlife worldwide and his understanding of animal habitats and their need to survive is second to none. His specialty is ethology, the scientific study of bird and animal behaviour – mainly how they interact and communicate. He has noticed – and has often told us – that many mammals set a good example by showing natural loyalty, kindness, responsibility and respect for their elders.

This doesn't stop sprites from making fun of how Mr Woodward can spit out his words in class when he gets over-excited by the animal he's discussing. When sprites ridicule his passion for wildlife and conservation, I wish I was brave enough to stick up for him and tell them to stop. I do hope courage will come when I begin to glow with my own colour. When this happens, I will attend special lessons with Miss Scaffold.

Miss Scaffold is highly proficient in safety procedures and provides rainbow-training classes in city centres up and down the country. I have never met her, but

I have heard that she shines the emerald green of harmony; she is straightforward, strict and a bit scary; and everyone does what she says. Miss Scaffold teaches sprites to listen out for the unique call nature sends for sprites to hold hands in the sky, which can also be detected by a smell in the air when it is just about to rain. We will have to practice and practice to learn the skill of balancing with other sprites to join forces with the rain and the sun's rays to form rainbows.

A few days after the Three Ws say we have to pass a test to go to the Nature Summit, word gets out that Miss Scaffold has been over-exposed to polluted air as a side-effect of her work and has become short of breath. Therefore, she has been recommended to stop giving these vital lessons altogether and move to recover in a woodland sanctuary where the air is pure and clean. The news spreads like wildfire from one sprite to another and causes a wave of panic.

"If Miss Scaffold stops teaching us, how will sprites learn how to make rainbows? Might they become a thing of the past?" I ask Miss Twig, who is in charge of our wellbeing, helping us develop the colour we'll shine.

"Shush," she says rather abruptly, putting a finger over her lips and frowning. "We don't want to cause alarm, do we? But..." – she lowered her voice – "between you and me, Woodland Welfare Workers all over the country are concerned about the bad gases polluting the air. This war against nature must stop, or much more than rainbows will disappear."

By the way, the glow that we sprites contribute to a rainbow comes from the energy we make that surrounds us. Miss Twig calls this our aura. Her aura is the sky blue of serenity and responsibility. It's a perfect colour match for her, as she is unflappable.

"Mmmm, I see," I murmur, not entirely understanding what she meant. I need to find out more about this 'war against nature', as Miss Twig put it, and the Nature Summit would be a perfect place to ask.

My worry is not that Anil and I might not pass the test to allow us to go, but that there won't be any spaces left for us. We still don't even know when we're going to take the test. I'd like to ask Robbie to reserve some spaces, but I haven't seen him around for ages. Whenever I see one of the Three Ws, I ask whether they've set a date for the test. All they say is that we need more time to study and must learn the value of patience. How can they say such a thing when the Nature Summit is getting so close?

The other day, there was a glimmer of hope about our potential trip. Miss Bracken set us a project to find something we hadn't noticed before, living on the forest floor, and study it. She called it coursework and said it was part of our test.

At first, all I could see was what I already knew: brown rotting leaves, insects and twigs. Miss Bracken warned us that we often only see what we expect to see and must learn to look further. Miss Bracken is what I would call crisp. She is sensible and matter-of-fact. She shines with the green of new beginnings, and instructs us about trees, shrubs, fungi and bacteria.

I squinted and squinted, and then there it was, right in front of my eyes – a massive patch of slime mould! Miss Bracken explained that slime mould is not a plant, nor an animal, nor a fungus. It lives in soil and is particularly fond of woodlands. The recent rainfall had encouraged it to grow, and I watched it creep several metres across the forest floor over the course of the day.

Anil watched the slime mould with me for a while and said it is sure to link up with and communicate through the Wood Wide Web underground. She showed me a type of fungus she had found. It wasn't a mushroom but another type of mould. It had grown over a dead mouse and had so far decomposed it down to its fur, transferring the nutrients from the little mammal back into the soil.

Miss Bracken was more than pleased and said that it takes a while for this type of mould to grow big enough for us to see and often goes about its business unnoticed. She's promised to put in a good word for us with Mr Woodward.

* * *

That weekend, I went camping in Cabilla Wood to learn new skills. The Three Ws had invited sprites from woodlands across the country for a sleepover in one enormous tent. I didn't know anyone. Anil wasn't included, and I wondered whether I was being put to some kind of test.

It's always nice to have at least one person you know

with you, and I was scared that I'd be picked on or laughed at, or that I just wouldn't fit in with the others. I thought about little else beforehand, even though part of me was looking forward to going.

When I arrived, a group of woodland sprites were sitting together around the campfire and had already made friends. They looked nice enough and I took my place among them.

"What pretty little flowers you're wearing in your hair," one says, using a sarcastic tone.

"We were about to play dare. I dare you to fly over the flames," says another.

"Of course she won't. You can see that she's not brave enough," says the next trying to taunt me.

"Actually," I answer without allowing myself to get upset, "I nearly gave it a try once."

"Scaredy-cat, scaredy-cat," another chants.

"I had been dared by some fireflies diving in and out of the flames," I say in an angry voice. "Luckily, just in time, something in my nature told me not to be so reckless.

I'm sorry to say they got very singed and needed more than walnut oil to recover their flight. Imagine being a firefly, let alone a woodland sprite without wings?"

That shut them up.

Determined to change the subject, I quickly think up a game and surprise myself by asking a question loud enough for everyone to hear.

"If you could be any animal, which one would it be, and why?"

"I'd be a badger," says one of the sprites right away. "I'd build myself a fantastic home just the way I like it and I'd fill my larder with all my favourite food."

Another says he would be a weaver bird, living in the forests of West Africa. He would weave a nest using his tiny beak just like we would use a needle and thread. "They're excellent at digging for insects with their beaks," he adds.

The game gradually develops into making and guessing animal sounds. I make a high-pitched cry, which some think is a gull. I try again, using a few helpful gestures, which makes everyone laugh, but my efforts are in vain. Eventually, I have to tell them that I was pretending to be a peregrine falcon flying through the air at two hundred miles an hour.

The games are easy enough to play, and make me forget my shyness.

As I stick a damp twig into a slice of sweet potato to cook it on the fire, I feel accepted, at ease and happy. I am pretty pleased, too, to have risen to the challenge of the taunting and had not allowed them to get the better of me.

We all eventually talk about Miss Scaffold. One sprite says he heard that her breathing was better since her rest and that she hoped to get back to work soon.

Then someone asks if we were granted three wishes, what would they be? I know mine right away, but I keep them to myself.

4

A DAY FULL OF NEWS

From the moment a newborn baby takes its first breath and cries, family members living in the spirit world summon a sprite to watch over the child as their fairy godparent. We flutter above the baby in their cot and sprinkle the finest fairy dust, mingled with the good wishes sent from the spiritual world by their ancestral relatives. Our godchild can see us clearly and hear our thoughts. We promise to guide them as best we can, teaching them to be kind to nature and each other, and to grow up happy within themselves. The baby shows that it understands by giving us its first smile. After performing this vital role, the spirit world sends us to live and work in the material world to look after nature. From then on, we uniquely connect with our own godchild through telepathy – by sending and receiving thoughts.

Anil and I have two godchildren; they're sisters exactly the same age as we are. They live in York, which happens not to be too far from the Temple of the Four Winds at Castle Howard. Although we have little hope of going, I couldn't resist sending a telepathic message to mine, and Anil did the same to hers. We said that we might be coming up and if so, we will arrange to play with them on Skelf Island at teatime on the day we arrive. I have learnt the value of planning ahead. After all, I would kick myself if we managed to go to York only to discover that they had accepted another invitation because we hadn't let them know.

* * *

I should be relieved because the day for our test has finally arrived, but instead, other things are troubling me. I fly down to talk them through with Anil.

"Are you ready for our test this afternoon?" I ask.

"Sort of," she says, hunching up her shoulders under her ears. "My new trick is learning the long names for things I look up in the library to bring them in wherever I can to score higher marks."

"That's clever," I say. "I've got a bit of bad news, I'm afraid," I add with a wavering voice. "Robbie told me that there are no more places left at the Temple of the Four Winds. Not for the ceremony, the dinner in the gardens, nor at the Nature Summit the next day. Not even room to hover." I feel tears well up in my eyes.

Anil flaps her wings to distract me. "I know, Sky. Don't worry, it's why Robbie's been avoiding us," she says without emotion. "He came to tell me how upset you are, but he's thought up a solution."

"There's no solution – apart from turning up and not being allowed in," I snap.

"Don't take it out on me. I'm just as upset as you are," says Anil pouting her lips and making a cross face. "Robbie explained about a newly discovered forest honeybee at Blenheim that we should ask the Three Ws to go and visit instead. They're smaller, furrier and darker than the ones we already know and are thought to be an ancient species."

"Blenheim?" I ask, bewildered.

"It's a palace where Robbie intends to stop off on his way back to Cornwall from the Nature Summit in Yorkshire and would be happy to meet us there to show us around."

"Bees at Blenheim, a palace?" I repeat. "It sounds wonderful, but I've set my heart on the Temple of the Four Winds – and seeing our godchildren too."

"You're always telling me that everything happens for a reason and that nine times out of ten, it's for a good one."

I return a weak smile. I know Anil is right and that we must do our best to keep courage.

We drink our herbal tea, eating a snack of peeled walnuts and dried plums. Dangling our feet over the edge of Anil's balcony, we enjoy the sun's warmth as it shines through the chilly autumn air and share thoughts between us without the need for words, and then head off, a little nervous, to take the test.

* * *

Later that day, the Three Ws summon Anil and me into our classroom to receive our test results. They are delighted to let us know that we have both passed with flying colours.

"Many congratulations," says Mr Woodward clapping his hands together. "You have excelled yourselves. I was particularly fascinated," he adds, beaming, "to read and learn about the Blenheim bees. Full marks."

Anil and I look at each other. "Come on, come on, you should be happy," he pauses, waiting for a response, but we are too stunned to give one. "What on earth's the matter with the two of you? Don't you want to go to the remarkable Temple of the Four Winds? Believe you me, it will be a fantastic experience. I wish I could have applied for tickets myself, but there's too much work to be done here. In any case, we're delighted that you will represent Cabilla at the Nature Summit and report full details back to us."

"That's all very well," I say with a sad voice. "But Robbie has suggested we meet him at Blenheim Palace on his way back from the Temple of the Four Winds to see the bees and play in the woods instead."

"But you've passed your test, so you'll fly up to the temple *with* Robbie. By all means, stop off with him on the way back. Bring us some of the honey to taste, too," he says buoyantly. "I'll let him know right away."

"It's too late, I'm afraid," I say, trying to put on a brave face.

"Oh no. Don't tell me that Robbie's left already. I wanted him to accompany you," he says with a heavy sigh.

"No, not that."

"What is it then, Sky?"

"Well," I say, "Robbie has told us that there are no more spaces left. The guest list filled up almost immediately, and there is nothing he can do about it to help."

"Oh, deary me," says Mr Woodward shaking his head vigorously in astonishment.

I take short breaths trying to calm my disappointment, but instead it brings on an onslaught of anger. I grit my teeth and fix fiery eyes upon him. The build-up of excitement had been high, but the letdown seemed worse than I could ever have imagined. I turn away, holding back my tears, pulling at Anil's sleeve, to head for the door.

But Mr Woodward makes a great fuss and waves his arms frantically around in the air to stop us, accidentally knocking things off the shelf behind him and making a tremendous amount of noise. "No, no, no," he says, spluttering out his words, lifting them to a crescendo, articulating every syllable. "You're setting off tonight! You go tonight! Yes, that's right. It's all sorted."

"But—" I begin.

"No buts about it! Naturally, I arranged for tickets immediately when we agreed you would go," interrupts Mr Woodward in a very loud voice. Stepping back, he pushes his fists into his sides, leans forwards and juts out his chin. "You don't honestly think that we'd put you through that rigorous test without already having the tickets reserved, do you? We had no doubt that you're both ready to set off on your first mission and adventure away from Cabilla," he said with a sense of finality and smiled triumphantly from ear to ear.

"And, another bit of good news," he adds. "You'll also enjoy the wedding of your old friend Barney, the barn owl from Bodmin, which is taking place before the dinner."

5

OUR ADVENTURE BEGINS

Once we realise that we are actually going to the gathering at the Temple of the Four Winds, we skip, jump for joy and do somersaults and pirouettes in the air. We go straight home to tidy up and prepare for our trip. Laying out a tray of leftovers from our larders, I take a break to sit on Anil's balcony and check that all was well with the woodland.

"Did you see how many nuts that grey squirrel over there buried to hide from the birds?" asks Anil, pointing towards the sweet chestnut tree.

"And from other squirrels," I say. "When they know they're being watched by a potential thief, they only pretend to bury their nuts."

I gaze out at our woodland. We flutter our wings to express our thanks for living here and show that we will miss our home and all our furry friends while we are away. I think about the laws passed to protect trees, animals and wildlife habitats. What puzzles me is why woodlands continue to be destroyed just when it suits a situation, like for a new motorway. I put a smudge on my hand to remind me to bring the subject up at the Nature Summit. The very thought makes me want to pinch myself that we are actually going and will be setting off this evening.

Before I head home up the rope ladder to get ready to leave, I carry the tray into Anil's kitchen, and we do the washing-up together. I empty tea leaves out of the teapot into Anil's compost bin, which hangs off the edge of her balcony. We add fresh food from her larder that we will have to leave behind. It will not go to waste – once invertebrates have broken it down to make soil, we will use it to nourish the seeds and herbs we grow in our vegetable patch in the fairy glade.

"Are you packed and ready to leave this evening?" I

ask. "It would be great to arrive by midday tomorrow, long before the party, so we have time to rest before we see our godchildren at teatime."

"Yes," she replies, clapping her hands together. "I'm so excited and have stuffed everything into my bag, including my waterproofs carefully folded around my dress."

* * *

While giving us details about our trip, the Three Ws tell us about their mounting concerns with the weather. In many parts of the world it is far too hot in the summer and much too icy in the winter. They fear that the changing climate may result in hurricanes and rainstorms uprooting trees, causing the land to wash into the sea; they worry that what has happened in other countries could happen to us.

The Three Ws stress that our mission is to build a network with a variety of nature sprites and fairy folk, not just from woodlands, but from all over the country and around the world.

"Tell the Four Winds," says Miss Twig, "that nature sprites in Cabilla will work for the common good by helping to gently calm them down. Make it clear that we all understand that their destructive behaviour is not their fault but a reaction to temperature changes outside their control."

"Take this report and read it with Anil this afternoon," Mr Woodward says, passing me a small booklet. "It's a record of destructive weather patterns here and abroad that you should know all about before you meet the Four Winds at their temple."

Miss Twig gives us a kind look. "You'll do fine," she says.

I smile.

"Use your time away to learn all that you can," adds Miss Bracken. "Listen carefully to everything said by the conservation warriors, but pay great attention to sprites telling their own experiences. Don't be afraid to ask questions. Listen and learn and you'll soon broaden your horizons."

"Thank you, Miss Bracken. Thank you, Miss Twig. And thank you for the book, Mr Woodward. You don't have to worry about us. And I promise to look after my little sister while we are away."

Now that we're heading off on our trip, I'm anxious that I'll waste the opportunity and have no idea what I'll do or say when I get there. I only know about life in Cabilla and worry that the international sprites will think I'm a country bumpkin without anything of interest to contribute.

Nothing drastic has ever occurred here that I can recall, but Mr Woodward reminded us that we had noted unsettling signs of erratic weather in our journals. I clutch the booklet with a sense of euphoria, determined to read it through with Anil before we leave. I'll listen to everyone I meet, and will be patient to find the true colour of my nature. I can feel something brewing towards it – when the moment comes along, I'll recognise something I really believe in, ready to run with it all the way to the finish line.

* * *

As the afternoon light turns to dusk and the day's blues, greys and whites gradually fade away, Anil climbs the rope ladder to step onto my balcony. We look out towards the river in wonder. Great groups of starlings fly in unison like schools of fish warding off predators. As the sun sinks in the distance, reds and oranges shine on the horizon. I see millions of stars and planets brighten in the twilight, dominated by the shining light of Venus.

It's time for us to go.

Setting off, we fly over our woodland to meet up with Robbie. We follow landmarks that are familiar to us, such as bushes on which we rely for food, birds' nests we have visited and our favourite evergreen trees. Nocturnal animals begin to emerge as the night deepens, many of whose habits we have studied and recorded in our journals.

I look down over Cabilla and notice a new den. It has been built by a hedgehog – I smile to myself with satisfaction as we have been encouraging him to do this for weeks. He's a quiet little creature that happily spends all day asleep rolled up in a ball, safe in the knowledge that the spines on his back will protect him from the claws and jaws of predators. I spot him moving shyly on his short legs, using his sense of smell to forage, eating as many beetles, caterpillars and earthworms as he can find. He is doing his best to put on weight so that he is ready to burrow into his cosy home for winter, where he will hibernate, sleeping without eating all winter long.

We pass above a badger we visited during the summer. He is dragging the mattress he has made from dry grasses, straw, bracken and dead leaves into the new underground burrow he has dug to share with his partner. He told us that he hopes she will produce a litter of cubs in early spring, and he is making sure that everything is ready.

Looking down from above, I realise that the ordinary animals and insects native to Cabilla have become my family. Life would not be the same without them and I will miss them while I'm away.

Soon we reach the fairy glade in the centre of the wood where the Woodland Welfare Workers live in their treehouses. Their auras can be seen glowing in varying shades of red, yellow, pink, green, orange, purple and blue from each window, showing that they are at home.

"I wish I was ready to make a rainbow with them," I say to Anil, gazing longingly at their bright colours radiating through the trees. Anil hunches her shoulders and spreads her hands to show that she has nothing more to say on the topic.

When we arrive at the spot where Robbie has arranged to meet us, he flies down, ready to guide us the rest of the way.

Robbie flies ahead, looking back at us from time to time to make sure we're keeping up. After a short while, we pass over Cabilla's secluded sanctuary at the furthest end of the woodland. The tranquility glides over me. Sprites that shine the blue of calm, the yellow of hope and happiness, or the green of new beginnings and abundance live in the sanctuary. I feel a little tingle of excitement run through me. It is where I will stay when I first find my colour to shine.

Until now, I have always felt my happiest when swimming in the beautiful still water of Siblyback Lake or Colliford reservoir. I love to float on my back, my ears listening to underwater sounds, looking up at the clouds as they move about the sky. Now looking down, flying over changing landscapes in the silence of the night feels just as wonderful and is an excellent time to think.

I look up at the stars twinkling in the moonlight,

reassured by their shine. I fly through the silent sky feeling at one with the Universe, connected to the harmony and rhythms of the moon. I ask the Universe to help me inspire those living on Earth to look after and love our planet. As I do so, a shooting star races past. I quickly close my eyes and make a promise to join with other sprites to create a kind world where everyone can live harmoniously with nature and each other.

6

SKELF ISLAND, CASTLE HOWARD

Our journey from the south of England to the north is as beautiful as it is tiring. Even so, Robbie suggests that we pass over Birmingham as a detour to see the destruction caused by a new train line. He says it is essential for us to witness the devastation in this ancient woodland for ourselves as it will help us speak up for displaced animals protesting at the temple.

We swoop down to take a closer look but find nothing but mud. Robbie was right. Hearing about it and seeing it in front of our eyes are two very different things. No animals are about. Robbed of shelter, any living creature is long gone. I can only hope that these animals are on their way to the Temple of the Four Winds to tell their story. Witnessing the devastation makes me all the more determined to help displaced animals and insects. But if they can't return to their homes, where can they go?

We arrive at Castle Howard at midday, having only stopped once in the early morning to eat and drink. The house and grounds are magnificent; I had never realised that bricks and mortar could be so elegant and represent such power. On the other hand, the guesthouse on Skelf Island where we will stay is not at all intimidating. It is charming and made of straw, accessed by a rope bridge – or, in our case, by air. There are two neat, identical bedrooms for Anil and me.

Exhausted yet exhilarated, we go straight to bed. Robbie takes a long rest in an empty bird box nearby. He will leave well before us this evening to interview spectators gathered around the temple for the service of thanksgiving.

Before settling, I flick through the pages of the book Mr Woodward gave me, which Anil and I read together before we left. I randomly stop to re-read how angry the weather has been behaving in different parts of the world, but then exhaustion grips me. I fall fast asleep, still holding the book in my hand.

* * *

I awake hours later to the sound of boisterous play and laughter. I fly up to the window in the roof to look outside. Our godchildren are running around in the afternoon sun, hugging trees tightly and playing with the skelves. Skelves have inhabited a secret world on Skelf Island for hundreds of years. These playful elf-like creatures are guardians of the island's wildlife, and are known for their love of nature – and their magic.

Children can only see sprites and fairies until they can talk. That's when they begin to sense us instead. Grown-ups can sense us, too, as long as they retain a youthful spirit. Sprites have lots of fun leaving clues to let children know when we are around. We might spray ourselves with flower water, or tickle children's cheeks with our wings. When there is a sweet scent lingering in the air, very different to the smell of perfume, and no flowers to be seen, you can be sure that sprites are around. Sometimes we leave little presents for our godchildren as a sign of our

affection for them – a feather, a shell, or a sudden shower of flower petals.

I fly into Anil's bedroom to wake her up.

"Are they already here?" she asks, sitting up excitedly and rubbing her eyes.

"Yes, come and see for yourself," I say. "They are frolicking in the garden with skelves – balancing on rope bridges, climbing and having fun."

We quickly spray ourselves with the sweet-smelling flower water on my dressing table and fly down to hide gifts all around the playground. Sensing our arrival, our godchildren wave hello and play tag with the skelves, howling with laughter. They love a scavenger hunt and compete against the skelves to look for the treasure we have hidden. Using telepathy, we give them clues, adding subtle signs to help the girls along, such as shaking leaves or imitating animal sounds near the hiding place. Anil's expertise is imitating a wolf howling. This ensures that they soon find everything, including the chocolate cupcakes we asked the food fairies to leave. When it is time for the girls to go home, they wave and blow us a kiss goodbye.

"Aren't they cute?" I whisper into Anil's ear. She nods, looking sad to see them leave.

"It's time to get a wiggle on and get dressed in our party togs," I say in a singsong voice, attempting to cheer her up. "I'm wearing the cornflower headdress I made. How about you?"

"Oh, lovely," she says with enthusiasm. "I packed my new hairband. It's a crown of ivy leaves that the fashion fairies made for me to keep my fringe off my face. Of course, that was before you cut it off," she laughs. "But before we get changed, please could we try out a new game? It popped into my head while I was resting."

"What kind of game?" I ask, not wishing to be late for the service at the temple.

"It's in two parts," says Anil. "First, you have to choose any letter from A to Z."

"Okay, I'll go for B, my favourite letter, because it's sort of symmetrical."

"Right," says Anil, clearly enjoying the game. "Now you need to name anything in the woods that begins with the letter B."

"That's harder than I thought," I reply, racking my brains. "Um … bugs. Bark beetles … blackbirds … barn owls … bats … bumblebees … butterflies … badgers … and beavers."

"Wow." says Anil, looking pleased with my answers.

"Now it's your turn," I say. "I bet I know which letter you'll select."

She replies straightaway. "Easy-peasy. A for ants."

I was right. I knew that I would be. Recently, Anil dedicated a double page in her notebook to a study of ants – which, during the summer, were building a nest in an old dead tree nearby. She spent ages watching them making repairs and fetching food, impressed by the way they worked together as a team without any arguments.

"Do we score a point for each answer?" I ask, wondering if she has thought this far ahead. "If so, you'll have to beat my total as you only have one point. But if you're quick, I'll give you a chance to think up a few more."

This is the kind of thing we often do together. Anil

gets an idea for a game and tells me all about it. As we play, we work out the rules. At other times, I think of an idea and mull it over with her before we share the new game with our friends.

Anil frowns, trying to think up more answers beginning with A. "I know," she says. "Apart from ants, we also watch over ash, alder, aspen and apple trees. We look out for acorns and pay attention to amphibians and all other animals."

I work out her score on my fingers. "That's eight points for you, and I get nine. But…" I add, "since you included the word 'all', I will award you a bonus point, and we'll call it a draw."

Delighted with the outcome, Anil claps her hands. I flap my wings in approval of the new game and fly into my bedroom to change into the beautiful dress I will wear to the temple. It's made of finely spun cotton embroidered with blue delphiniums and pink rose petals, sewn with a sprinkling of golden linseed.

Anil has packed a long-sleeved dress made from autumn leaves, and with a collar made of ivy. It has a border of lichen around the hem and cuffs with three bright red berry buttons at the neck. She has kept it in the cedar chest in her bedroom for ages and ages, ready for a special occasion.

As soon as Anil is dressed, she goes out onto the rope bridge through the hall to look for something pretty to add to her headdress.

I watch as the sun sinks slowly behind the horizon, and a deer paws the ground at the base of a tree behind our guest house. Munching on moss, the deer disturbs a roost of miniature red admiral butterflies, which rise up, caught by the wind. I step out onto the rope bridge just in time to see the butterflies settle on Anil's headdress.

Anil is radiant. She has always loved the beautiful wings of the red admiral, which have symmetrical dark brown, orange and black patterns. They're the perfect decoration and match the autumn leaves of her dress. "You'll never guess what just happened," she whispers. "I was thinking about what I could use to decorate my headdress when the butterflies flew around me as if they had heard my thoughts."

I'm fascinated by Anil's description of her telepathic experience with butterflies. This kind of connection is usually reserved for sprites and their godchild or between each other, but never with other species. We know that trees use a language unique to them, so perhaps we can tune in to that too? Anil and I constantly try but always seem to fail. Maybe we just aren't trying hard enough.

The ceremony at the Temple of the Four Winds beside Ray Wood is only a few minutes' flight from our lodgings. Our escort, Charlie, a chaffinch wearing a festive grey and blue cap, has been looking out for us from a tall pine tree where he roosts, close to our lodgings. Charlie is very chatty as we set off. Flying above Ray Wood, he tells us all about the mysteries of the wood. He confides that he has perched on a branch of a magical yew tree in the centre of the wood, which is over a thousand years old, and made a wish to meet his soulmate. I marvel at the yew tree, and then only a moment later, I see what we came all this way for.

"There it is," he says, gliding down to our destination. "The Temple of the Four Winds, built to acknowledge their great power. Its porticos represent the

North, South, East and West Winds, facing all four directions."

The magnificent temple is decorated with sculptures and pillars on each of the four sides forming porticos at the top of four sets of steps. It is a perfect square, with four doors opening into a single room in the middle, and is set on top of a hill, with panoramic views. I can instantly see the reason for building it on high ground – there's nothing to get in the way of the Winds in any direction for miles around.

7

GIVING THANKS

Anil and I thank Charlie for guiding us to the beautiful Temple of the Four Winds. He tweets a friendly goodbye before leaving us to join his friends at the juice bar.

I send a *staccato* thought to Anil. These are quick messages as precise as musical notes to communicate short explanations in code. I share my feeling of being left on our own and finding it intimidating. Anil replies with a humorous image she has made up on the spot, alarmed caricatures of us in a crowd, making the joke that we are not exactly alone. And she's right – there are literally masses of fairies flying above, below and around us with others on foot too.

We hover, a little perplexed, above the imposing temple and watch goblins, pixies and leprechauns dressed in vibrant variations of green trudge through soggy grass. Many nature sprites and fairies fly alongside, some at their shoulders, arriving with determination from every direction.

As twilight begins to fall into darkness, impish, playful fairies fly about, lighting candles, illuminating the stone statues. The statues are similar to those from ancient Rome, standing elegantly and silently at the top of each flight of steps. They safeguard the temple at the four entrances on each side and welcome visitors who make the climb to the top. But the firmly closed doors let us know that we must remain outside until we are invited in.

"Let's fly to the steps and wait for the doors to open," I suggest, my heart fluttering with nervous excitement.

We fly down and join the crowd to take our turn in the enormous queues. Many fairy sprites fly about greeting each other and have evidently met before. I stand steadfast with Anil on the west side of the temple, hardly moving, unsure of what we are waiting for. I look up at the sky. It is very still, clear of clouds, full of stars and beautifully lit by the moon. Then I feel a warm, gentle breeze whisper a welcome. I recognise this as the voice of the West Wind, which sends the mildest breeze to encourage us towards the steps, herding guests into an enormous circle, as a sheepdog would round up its flock. Any anxiety I may have felt beforehand lessens as I manoeuvre towards the steps, holding hands with my sister.

There are now hundreds of us surrounding the temple. A hush sweeps through like a wave, and we remain as quiet as can be. We are waiting. Waiting.

Suddenly, out of nowhere, the cold North Wind arrives over the north side of the temple. It is a magnificent and dramatic performance, the North Wind changing before our eyes, taking on the form of a dense, dark cloud in the shape of a wolf. The fast-moving wolf cloud takes an enormous breath, only to blow it out in one sharp blast, crashing open the north door to the temple. Then, howling to the heavens, the North Wind summons the East, West and South Winds to show themselves.

Within moments, the warm South Wind appears out of nowhere, as a cloud shaped like a lion. Its loud roars open the south door. A slow rumble follows from the east, and a quick-moving cloud in the form of a tiger appears, illuminated by a flash of lightening, leaping through the dark sky. It is the East Wind. Seconds later, the east door is thrown open by a crash of thunder.

The three Winds fall silent and settle around the central dome, looking down at us. Stunned, spectators hardly dare breathe or disturb the moment. I squeeze Anil's hand tight. Whatever will come next? Soon, I pick up a whirling sound building in the sky. I look up to see the West Wind spiralling higher and higher. I crane my neck to watch as it climbs. It is no longer recognisable as the gentle breath that greeted us moments ago. Instead, it hovers like a cloud, miles above the temple, in the familiar shape of a peregrine falcon, the fastest animal on Earth. The falcon cloud dives from the heavens, its wings tucked in, hurtling towards the west door, pushing it open with its hooked beak. The falcon swoops through the open door, into the building and out again, then floats triumphantly above the portico protecting the terrace at the top of the west steps.

The Winds rise up and join each other to blow all around us, almost knocking us over. Flapping and spreading its wings wide, the West Wind invites us to enter the building. I see each Wind sending a breeze to give visitors a gentle nudge up their stairs. Then, instantaneously, we are surrounded by stillness, as though a switch has been flicked off. The Four Winds have entered their temple, where they will be invisible to us, leaving the four doors open wide ready for us to enter.

In awe of the remarkable display of power, Anil and I stand and wait our turn in the queue. Guests silently mount the steps in front of and behind us. Reaching the top, Anil and I release hands and enter through the west door.

Four male fairies resembling beautiful Roman gods, dressed in robes similar to those worn by the statues around the temple, hover above the four doors.

"Welcome," says the fairy at the west entrance. "The thanksgiving is about to begin. Titania, Queen of the fairies, will introduce the ceremony as soon as you are all settled."

The room is beautiful. The four entrances are framed with dark marble pillars; the floor, patterned and inset with precious stones. Decorated panels are embedded into the walls above the doors and around a circular glass dome in the centre. Antique, wooden benches form squares of seating around a large mosaic in the middle resembling a chessboard below the dome. There's a great bustle as we take our seats. Sprites and fairies also find places to hover in layers all the way up to the ceiling.

Fashion fairies have been very busy making fabulous clothes for the occasion, which Anil and I admire – long cloaks, fitted dresses and bodices sewn with flowers. Others wear petal skirts, britches, jackets or plain tops with elaborate lacing. A hum echoes through the room. It is a sound made by fairies of shared happiness. It is similar to the hum made by hummingbirds when they hover in front of flowers to feed.

From smiles passed between fairies, it is evident that telepathic messages are being sent all over the place and I feel the strength of positive energy all around.

Sitting on the wooden bench in the temple, unsure

of my purpose, the West Wind blows gently through my hair and around me as if checking me out. It is a strangely calming, comforting, cooling sensation. A sense of bliss that passes through me, washing away my doubts.

Anil nudges me. Titania, Queen of the fairies, wearing a long, white satin gown and a crystal crown, takes her place under the dome where everyone can see her hover. The elegant fairy bows her head respectfully, first towards the North Wind, then to the South Wind followed by the East and West Winds, slowly patting the air with her hands, indicating that it is time for the ceremony to begin.

"Oh, mighty Winds, your power is immense," says Queen Titania. "We give thanks to you for all the good that you do to help us look after our planet. We pledge to help calm you by cleaning the air to halt the warming temperatures that have angered you so very much. Tomorrow, nature sprites will gather here together for the Nature Summit and share stories so that you, as well as all of us, can understand what needs to be done to help calm you and the weather at the four corners of the world. And to stop the destruction caused to so many lives.

"Nature sprites sailing with their godchildren from some of the areas most affected by the climate crisis will tell their stories outside the temple, asking for our help. I have received many telepathic messages and have chosen to gather these together to reflect the shared wisdom from sprites protecting nature around the world:

"When the last woodland is cut and sold, there will be no shade beneath the beating sun for anyone. The birds will breathe foal air, with no song or place to perch. The fish will no longer swim along rivers run dry. It will be too late when they say it's time to put things right. When no rain falls upon the arid land, no chests of gold can fix what has already been done.

"Yet our minds are set with hope. Yes, the Four Winds require our nurture to make things right. But together, with determination, we will find a way.

"Let us give thanks to the Four Winds."

A calm wind of approval briefly wafts around the room and then is gone. We are left to sit in silence to give thanks in our way. I think about creatures under my care in the woodland and the remarkable unseen work done by microorganisms that help everything to run smoothly behind the scenes. I bow my head. I give thanks for the moon and stars that shine so brightly; for the sun that warms the cold air and makes seeds grow; for rivers that flow like veins through our lands to bring water, provide transportation, produce electricity, to swim in and go boating. I thank the Universe for our great oceans, the lakes, mountains, rain and – most of all – my ability to understand problems with a capacity to do something about them.

With a sense of unity between us, we embrace each other without the need to communicate in any other way other than sharing the positive energy in our auras.

The four robed fairies hovering at each door break the silence.

"Thank you for coming to show your appreciation," they say in unison. "We will host the Nature Summit tomorrow on behalf of the Four Winds. In the meantime, please find your way down the steps and to the garden party where the wedding of two barn owls will take place." Each gives a respectful nod and we follow their lead and find our way out into the fresh air.

8

A CELEBRATION

"Whoopee!" says Anil, looking around, enchanted. Beeswax candles in lanterns are everywhere – they hang from trees and are set out on tables, too. Glow-worms illuminate walkways with ribbons of light. Every local woodland creature, big and small, seems to be there. They mill around looking their smartest, chatting. I spot a wild turkey and a goose, a mouse with a hare, a badger talking to a fox, and a hedgehog all on its own.

The food fairies dart about, welcoming guests, guiding them to tables, and handing out appetisers served on woven wicker trays. There are pickled pixie pears wrapped in leaves that have been soaked in maple syrup and upturned bellflowers filled with morning dew, sweetened with honey.

"Delicious," we say, helping ourselves, and fly off to the broad branch of an alder tree, the perfect place to perch with a great view of the tree hollow where the wedding ceremony of the barn owls will be held.

A magpie, smart in her glossy black and white plumage, steps out in front of the assembled well-wishers. She carries two golden rings in her beak. The rings are special: they each contain a tracking device so that Barney and Brownie can be followed after their honeymoon to check that Brownie, who has always lived in a barn and only recently came to the hollow, has settled in her new habitat.

Fayetta, a French flower fairy and the maid of honour, comes out of the hollow where she has been attending to Brownie, and carefully takes the rings from Maggie's beak. She wears a beautiful dress embroidered with pansies, pinks and primroses, sewn with silkworm silk, and carries a basket of rose petal confetti over her arm. Barney perches outside the hollow, waiting. Then Brownie emerges from the hollow. The hollow is strewn with straw and white clover flowers, which smell faintly of honey. Fayetta places the rings around the owls' ankles to symbolise their commitment to each other.

As Fayetta sprinkles rose petal confetti into the hollow to bless the couple, Maggie pronounces them married. Maggie's partner, Marvin, who is sitting further along the same branch, announces that they will sing a duet, a folk song about magpies.

One's for sorrow,
Two's for joy,
Three's for a girl and
Four's for a boy.
Five's for silver,
Six for gold,
Seven's for a secret never to be told.
Eight magpies for a wish,
Nine for a kiss,
Ten a surprise never to miss.
Eleven for health,
Twelve for wealth!

"And," adds Marvin, gesturing towards the couple,

"*stealth* to help them catch a nutritious dinner."

A fanfare, consisting of guests hooting, chirping, clapping and stamping their feet, follows the magpies' song. The sounds reverberate through the woodland into the still night.

Barney and Brownie perch on the edge of the hollow, looking around at their guests. "Thank you, Mr and Mrs Magpie. And thank you all for being here to share in our celebration," Barney says with a nod and a wink, turning his head from right to left. "Those who do not know me may wonder why Brownie and I have not settled in a barn – which is, after all, where barn owls prefer to nest. But anyone who knows me will know that I moved to this hollow a while ago due to difficult circumstances that I had not foreseen." Barney turns his head around again out of habit – he's keeping an eye out for predators.

"The barn that has been my family home for many generations, on the edge of Bodmin Moor, was recently restored to make a home for people. Forced off my ancestors' land in Cornwall, I flew away in distress. I headed north and ended up close to the Yorkshire Moors, where I was fortunate enough to meet Brownie.

"On this, our wedding day, I can honestly say that, although there were times when I was close to despair, everything has changed for the better. I am much wiser for the experience, and now have a home on this lovely estate where I have made a nest with my beautiful Brownie. I am proud to announce to you all that we will be raising a family in the new year."

The crowd cheers.

"Please enjoy your party tonight celebrating nature and eat to your hearts' content," he concludes.

Voles and mice exchange worried looks, unsure whether the owls have invited them to the feast – or to be feasted upon.

Barney hoots at the musicians, who have assembled in the clearing below. Fairies mingle among us to announce that music will be played throughout the evening on pixie pipes and fiddles. Leprechauns and fairies will also perform mimes, sing folk songs and tell fables.

I nod to an older fairy sitting beside me – a mark of

respect that a young sprite is expected to show to their elders. She is beautifully dressed in a long skirt, top and a short jacket in shades of peach, cream and brown. She says hello. Her name is Bella. She is an artist who paints the beauty of nature around the world. I tell her my name, and explain that I have arrived from Cabilla and this is my first time away.

"Ah, Cornwall. A county rich with Celtic heritage." She smiles, looking towards the newly married couple. "It's so lovely that Barney's story has a happy ending!" she adds. "This tree has witnessed the weddings of so many owls. Some have been happy, some have been raucous, some have been quiet. Yet what really matters is that each new couple loves and cares for each other." With a smile, Bella excuses herself to join the high table, where she is a guest of honour.

From the shelter of their hollow, the bride and groom have a perfect view of the celebration. Design fairies have decorated a high table with flower arrangements from one end to another using woodland colours – whites, greys, greens and browns.

Wedding tunes played by groups of musicians create a joyful atmosphere. As birds join in with the singing, the holly and rowan offer their red berries, silver birch, ash, yew and beech trees throw their seeds as part of the festivities. Bats feast upon the insects and grubs hiding behind tree bark or fluttering around, hoping not to be detected by their predators.

Jugs of fermented hops and pressed berry juice have been placed on tables. Guests waving tickets to attend the seated dinner flock around the tables. Budskap, the Master of Ceremonies, hops up onto a podium, holds up a gong, hits it decisively with a stick and announces, "Please take your seats. Dinner is about to be served."

9

NEW FRIENDS

I hadn't realised that tables could fill up quite so quickly. A food fairy beckons Anil to sit at one reserved for budding conservationists. I am lucky to find an empty place at one of the toadstool tables and join a short, thickset goblin with a light green complexion. I recognise him from the service at the temple. I have never made friends with a goblin before, but for some reason I feel drawn to him.

He welcomes me by politely standing up, pulling out the spare chair for me so that I can perch comfortably on it. "Good evening," he says. "My name is Kobalos. I'm a goblin whose ancestors immigrated to England from Greece a very long time ago."

"How do you do?" I say. "My name is Sky."

"I'm very pleased that you came to sit with me," he says, and proceeds to tell me how he has enjoyed the evening so far.

Some folk still dislike goblins because of all the fairy tales about them, which show goblins as mischievous, greedy for gold and often evil. But as I listen to the goblin, I watch his face and pick up his aura, which Miss Twig has taught me to do. I can see that he has no trace of malice. On the contrary, he is gentle and kind, appears perfectly content, and seems to be sensitive and clever. I tell him that he has rare qualities. Clearly unused to compliments, Kobalos almost chokes on his drink.

"Goodness!" he exclaims with a grin, exposing a set of uneven green-tinged teeth. His breath, I notice, smells of sweet hay. "Goblins, as you know, are not like sprites. Our energy is hidden, whereas sprites show their character in the colour of their glow, once they have found them, of course. So how will you achieve your unique colour?"

"To be honest, I'm not quite sure. I've been told that it will happen when I settle down into my true nature and show myself as entirely genuine. My teachers say it helps if we try to see ourselves as who we really are, and as who we could be. I have been through many stages, including being disobedient, stubborn, fearful and sometimes quite rude. But when my teachers can see that I am behaving true to myself, I will be put to a final test."

"Oh," says the goblin hovering an elbow above an apple lying on the table, pushing a finger up into his chin. He raises an eyebrow. "What kind of test?" he asks.

"It's not like a school test," I explain. "One of my teachers, Miss Twig, says that we will only find our true nature when we behave genuinely towards others. Spirits of the air watch for signs that we are kind and generous, and decide whether our acts of kindness and compassion are genuine or pretend."

"That makes sense," says Kobalos. "It's an important lesson to learn that nobody, whoever they are, can hide from the truth. Truth has a habit of shining through whether you're looking for it or not, especially where nature is concerned."

"I often find solutions to problems in nature," I say.

"I agree. After all, you cannot invent truth; only lies are invented," Kobalos tells me.

"My teachers said to listen and learn from others," I say, looking him in the eye. "Do you have any clues that will help me on my way?"

"Well, let me see," he says, pausing for thought. "Solutions are the only thing that really matter in the end, whatever the problem, and the integrity of doing good for others as there is nothing more rewarding than helping those in need."

"I agree," I say, nodding my head.

"One last tip," he says, "Make sure that you don't lose track of what it is you're aiming for. Patience is power, and never forget that you will only achieve what you set out to achieve if you believe that you can."

We clink our cups together as a mark of good cheer.

"Valuable," I say, showing high respect. Remembering that it's selfish to only talk about myself, I change the subject. "What is your connection with nature? I don't mean to be rude, but I wondered about your green fingers – I've heard they can help with growing vegetables?" I ask.

"Ah, you're not that far off," Kobalos laughs. "I had never thought of that before. But, you may be surprised to hear that I used to dig coal and was trained as an apprentice in the pixie kingdom, which, as you may know, is very small. I was lucky to work in the mines – goblins are famous for being skilled miners and experts in tunnelling."

"But what about the bad effects that burning mined coal has on the air we breathe?" I ask.

"Ah yes, that is of great concern," answers Kobalos, to my double surprise. "The mine where I used to work closed down a few years ago and I learnt that burning coal, a fossil fuel, is harmful, creating gases that warm the climate. The same goes for burning oil and gas, and the whole issue is a worrying one, but not without solutions."

"The iron that's used to make steel is dangerous to fairies," I say. "It can block our magic. On top of that, burning coal makes us breathless."

"I know," he replies. "After the mine closed down, I tried to find another job, but the boss in charge told me that mining coal was the only work I'd be any good at." He hunches his shoulders, rapidly shaking his hands around from left to right in front of him. "But, what would he know about *me* better than *myself*, let alone what I'm capable of? So I set off to explore my own possibilities and follow my dreams. When we start believing in ourselves, we soon find out that we're capable of many things."

"Oooh," I say, "That's so encouraging. But aren't goblins also famous for their skill at making hammers, pickaxes, swords, needles, daggers and tongs?"

"Indeed we are," replies Kobalos, lifting his chin, looking pleased. "Metal-working has always been my passion, but don't forget that coal is one of the few minerals that burns hot enough to manufacture the steel required to make these tools."

"Of course," I say, realising my error.

"So what did you do?" I ask.

"A year ago, a man came knocking at my door. He offered me some gold to dig coal to burn and make steel. But, because burning coal damages our environment, I said no. The next day the man returned and offered me even more gold to do the same work. That would have made me rich, but again I said no.'

"You definitely did the right thing," I say.

"Yes, I was pleasantly surprised that, put in a situation like that, I discovered that I would not be swayed by greed."

"And you had concern for others," I add.

"It led me to think about what is precious apart from friends and family."

"What is?" I ask.

"Three things," says Kobalos. "Freedom to live honestly, integrity to face the truth and contentment from helping others."

"Did it help your dreams come true?" I ask.

"Yes," he says. "I now work on rewilding projects as a volunteer for the Woodmeadow Trust. I tend trees and aid pond life, scarify the soil, planting new trees and the understory below their canopy to provide an important balance in our ecosystem. I am sure you know that there is much, much more than just planting trees to create havens for wildlife?"

I nod enthusiastically. "I watch pollinators thrive on the succession of flowers through seasonal trees, shrubs and wildflowers that connect me with the seasons. When they fade away and disappear, I can hardly believe it when they reappear like magic along with the sounds, scents and songs their flowers attract to the woodland."

Kobalos nods in recognition. "I am also an apprentice to Pol, a pixie sculptor creating artworks that soothe the spirit. I hammer out old steel car body parts, which Pol transforms into magnificent sculptures. He places these in among the trees, where the polished surfaces of the sculptures reflect the changing faces of nature throughout the seasons. Working with my hands in these two very different ways has led me to reach a level of personal contentment that is beyond my wildest dreams."

"Class!" I say, admiring his ability to change things for the better.

"Not everyone has the chance or the courage to follow their dreams. But, of course, the underlying issue is often that life isn't always fair."

"Can it ever be fair?" I ask, thinking about the animals having to flee their woodland homes through no fault of their own.

"No, but it can still be good," Kobalos says with a knowing nod. "When we learn to accept ourselves, to be responsible for our actions and to care for each other, we can become our best selves. It's no good complaining that life would have been better if things had been different. No, life is what we make of it. It is better to be content with what we have and who we are, instead of moaning and wanting something else."

"Miss Twig says that we should create increasingly difficult targets for ourselves – and that fits in with what I'd like to do," I say.

"What's that?" he asks.

"To do something that will help nature thrive, especially wildlife and the Four Winds. But I've no real idea of what I can do to make a difference."

"Be ambitious and reach for the stars, Sky. When

you focus and have a vision of what it is you want, every triumph, however small, will join up with all your other achievements to grow into something you are aiming for. Gather remarkable people around you to help you achieve your mission. Believe you me, global temperatures rising are a challenge placed before us, ready to be overcome," Kobalos smiles.

"Worthy!" I cry out with enthusiasm. "I'm worried about tomorrow, of making the most of the Nature Summit and doing something to help displaced animals. Apparently they're ready to be as disruptive as possible in protest."

"You can't carry all the problems of the world on your own shoulders, Sky. Use your time here to listen, learn and respond. Outside nature, there's too much grey in the world, with everyone supposed to act the same, think the same, react in the same way and be afraid to say what they mean. The fact that you are thinking about saving the animals will attract an opportunity for you to help them. When your time comes, I am sure you will be an inspiration to others and hope that you will add a little colour to brighten up other people's lives and make the world a better place."

"That's nice. Thank you, Kobalos," I say, wondering how on earth I will go about finding new homes for disrupted creatures.

Out of the corner of my eye, I notice a small, neat pixie at Bella's table taking a partner for a dance. I recognise her from a picture in the *Weekly Woodland News* – a conservation warrior named Lydia. She was interviewed after she witnessed heavy rains uprooting trees and flooding rivers during the spring.

"Who's that?" I ask, pointing at the pixie Lydia is dancing with.

"Oh, he's a pixie prince named Pascal," Kobalos says, waving at Bella, who's sitting at the high table. "I'll introduce you, if you like. To his family's horror, he abandoned his palace, wealth and kingdom to find freedom living on a boat with his books. He now sails the high seas, experiencing the wonders of the world."

Pascal, looking upset, returns to the table.

"Come back soon, Lydia," he calls. "I would like to

see you again."

Kobalos suggests that we join Prince Pascal and Bella at their table. Pascal sees us making our way over and beckons to us.

I curtsy to the pixie prince. Able to pick up the royal purple in his aura, it's easy to see he's of noble blood. There's an orange sheen to the outer edge, though, which I associate with transformation. He must have acquired this when he left his kingdom, lands, power and wealth behind him and began to live a more simple life.

"Hello, my friend," says Pascal, clapping Kobalos on the back "And mademoiselle," he bows to me. "It is with delight that I welcome a nature sprite to my table," he says with a charming pixie accent. His face is a mass of deep lines, and he is smartly dressed in clothes that smell of the sea.

Kobalos excuses himself to join Bella, who's sitting at the other end of the table.

"I hear you live on a boat?" I say to Pascal.

"Yes. I'm so lucky to enjoy the wind in my sails," he

says, giving me a wink. His eyes are kind and full of humour. "I have had the good fortune to change my life and live with nature, as I assume you do. I have found this to be much more rewarding than the status and responsibility of wealth, which became a burden to me. I find that family, friendships, beauty and serenity are more important than wealth and power."

"Travelling by boat must be full of adventure," I say. "How did you get here?"

"Well," he says, looking pleased to have been asked. "I followed a network of rivers from the North Sea to Mill Hills Beck. I moored my boat, *Trade Winds*, beside the three arches here at New River Bridge. And I will return the same way I came, to sail the high seas." He raises his glass to me. "May I come to see you before I set sail on my next adventure?"

"With pleasure," I reply. "We're staying in a straw guesthouse on stilts among the trees on Skelf Island." I point in the direction of our lodgings. "I look forward to introducing you to my sister, Anil. That reminds me – I must try to find her."

10

TAKEN BY STORM

I say goodbye to Pascal, wave to Kobalos and Bella, and fly up into a tree to have a better view of the guests. Soon I spot my sister peering into a pond. I fly down to join her.

She is studying a frog. I look into the frog's big, bulging, translucent eyes and he gives a loud croak. Next, the frog's long sticky tongue shoots out to snatch a snail. Before the poor creature can see it coming, the frog has swallowed the snail, shell and all.

"What a way to catch a meal," says Anil to the frog.

"It was not very polite of me, I know," he replies. "We frogs have no teeth, so we have to swallow our food whole." The frog burps loudly and hops off to look for another snack. Anil and I flutter up to a low tree branch to watch the festivities.

A leprechaun dressed in green shamrock leaves stands on a toadstool table. He announces the cutting of the wedding cake. At the same time, cups are topped up before the entertainment begins. There is clapping and cheering. To draw the audience's attention back to him, the leprechaun whistles and everyone quietens down.

"I am honoured to have been invited by nature sprites to say a few words to prepare such eminent fairy folk for the Nature Summit tomorrow," the leprechaun says. "You may have noticed from my accent and from the way I dress that I am an Irish leprechaun. My name is Liam, and I am pleased to wear Ireland's national emblem, the shamrock. The four-leafed clover is a rare variation of the three-leafed clover, and people consider it a symbol of good luck, faith, hope, and love."

Looks and smiles are shared between the listeners.

"I only mention this because we need all the luck in the world right now to help nature bring back the colour into its cheeks and to care for it with love and attention. At the Nature Summit tomorrow, we will hear stories told of the troubles faced by sprites around the world. This gathering of like-minded fairy folk is an opportunity to help turn problems around.

"This work depends on group determination to make things right. After all, it's easier to destroy a house than it is to build one." He pauses for thought, not taking his eyes off the crowd. "It takes courage to fight for a good cause. But, so many things are possible," he says, pulling himself up. "The one thing I'm absolutely certain about is that where there's a will, there's a way."

The crowd cheers again.

As I clap my hands, Anil gets down from the tree branch and puts her ear to the ground.

"What are you doing?" I ask.

"I can feel a rumbling underground. I heard it earlier, but now it's much stronger. I think the trees are sending a warning to each other through their roots and the Wood Wide Web. I can't quite hear what they're saying to each other because the sounds are new to me, but I can tell that the vibrations are coming from miles away – even as far south as Cabilla."

I join Anil and kneel on the ground. I still can't hear the sounds she mentions; only the guests making noise all around us. They are dancing, laughing, singing, all swept away by the euphoria of the evening.

Without warning, the ferocious ice-cold North Wind sweeps through the trees. Candlelight goes out, flicked off in a single breath. Next, a gusty wind joins in from the west, warmer but no less vicious. Then comes a turbulent wind from the east, quickly followed by a fierce wind from the south. Together, the Four Winds blow so violently that the musicians are forced to stop playing. They drop their instruments and fall to the ground. The Winds whistle through flutes and pixie pipes, making loud, angry sounds, seizing fiddles and twirling them through the air, only for them to crash to the ground. Elven harps are snatched out of the musicians' hands and sent flying. The rain lashes out, coming down hard, splashing off every surface. Players run for shelter, tripping over roots, rushing to take cover. Bushes rustle with warning, blown this way and that.

Liam is thrown to the ground, skids in the mud and

rolls towards the lake looking for anything to hold onto. Anil grabs a twig and clings to it to save herself from being blown away. The butterflies, hibernating in her headdress, lose their grip. They flap their delicate wings as best they can, but are taken by the wind.

I see Bella huddled up with Lydia, protected by a cluster of mushrooms. Fayetta, still carrying her basket, beckons to Maggie and Marvin to quickly join Barney and Brownie in their hollow. Wet with rain, Maggie peeps out, looking very sorry to see that the party has come to an abrupt end.

Insects and animals scramble to take refuge, running into nests, climbing up trees, escaping into underground dens. Spiders and earthworms dive into the soil or cling to tree roots, bark and shrubs to protect themselves against the harsh wind. It is like a terrifying game where each player is looking frantically for somewhere safe, fighting against the force of the weather all at the same time.

As I clutch the sturdy stem of an evergreen bush, I am relieved to see that owls and bats have hidden in the hollows of trees. Other guests hang on to whatever branch or shrub they can find so they are not blown away.

With a sense of foreboding, I recall the notes I recorded in my journal. I wrote that this autumn there had been far more rain than usual in Cabilla, and that the ground had become waterlogged, with potentially disastrous consequences to woodland trees and surrounding areas. Storms with heavy rainfall had caused the river on the far side of the wood to burst its banks and overflow onto the floodplain more than once. But, as I hold on tight to the evergreen bush, listening to the wind, I realise that Anil was right about the warning she picked up from the tree roots: this storm is huge.

I worry that trees will struggle to keep upright against the violent force of nature. Leaves are stripped off the trees by the fierce Winds, and I shiver. My intuition tells me that this is no random storm. No – the Four Winds are making a stand at their temple and throughout the country; their timely protest against climate change when we're right here to listen.

Although some wedding guests cannot speak the language of the wind and the rain as sprites can, they hear the Four Winds' angry message loud and clear. As ferocious clouds form in the dark sky, I pick out animal shapes casting their shadow, an encore to their earlier performances, but this time without their earlier restraint. A wolf, howling, growling and snarling, leaps across the sky from north to south. Next comes a lion from the south, and a cloud in the shape of a tiger from the east. Moments later, there's a flash of lightening and a deep rumble of thunder, then a cloud shaped like a falcon swoops in from the west, this time with its wings and talons outstretched. Each cloud creature is crying out to us for help. *If the disrespect for nature continues,* I hear the Four Winds scream, *we will lose our ability to prevent glaciers melting, cause bush fires, unleash torrential rains and generate flash floods.*

I try to keep calm. There's nothing we can do for now but hold on tight to whatever we can and wait for the weather to settle down.

But the Four Winds gain momentum. As they do so, Anil cries out for help. The twig she is clinging to is about to snap. I reach out and catch her just in time, scooping her up and grasping her firmly by the hand. But in the process, I lose grip on my secure stem.

Kobalos leaps to his feet from a sheltered position between two large tree roots reaches up towards me and manages to grab my other hand by the wrist. As he tries to pull us back down to safety, Liam sways violently back and forth, and loses his hold on a tall reed, catapulting towards us. Liam just manages to catch Pascal's tailcoat, who had been holding fast to a tree. Keen to help, the pixie prince grabs Kobalos by the arm, but soon we are all carried away by the strong Winds together.

Lightning strikes a jagged scar through the sky over the Temple of the Four Winds. The storm rumbles like drums, and the lightning looks ready to crack the sky open. We hang on to each other, left to the mercy of the gale-force wind. Then, Anil, Kobalos, Pascal, Liam and I are dragged upwards in a tornado, pulled higher and higher, swirling and circling upwards.

It happens so fast. I promise the Four Winds to protect them with all my might – if only they will take us to safety.

I close my eyes tightly, hoping for the best, and call out into the darkness. "Hold on, Anil. Don't let go!"

11

THE YEW TREE

Anil and I awake to an eerie calm. It's morning. We're on the branch of a tall yew tree, surrounded by thick clouds. Kobalos is hanging from the lapel of his jacket, which is caught on a sprig of ivy beside us. I lean over and help him break free.

"Thank you," he says, pulling a cotton handkerchief from his top pocket to mop up the raindrops flicked onto his face by the ivy leaves. "What a remarkable journey."

"How did we get here?" I ask. "I can't remember a thing about it."

"Nor me," says Anil. "I remember being terrified

and having a strange dream. Your voice in the darkness was the only reason I managed to keep hold of your hand and not let go."

"As soon as the storm calmed down," Kobalos tells us, "the West Wind came to our rescue. Again, it took the form of a falcon and carried us on its back to settle us here. It was, without a doubt, close to a miracle."

"So you saw the falcon too," says Anil. "I thought it was just a dream."

Looking around through the cloud, I see Liam and Pascal. They are draped on branches above us, their shirt tails dangling down, like washing on a line. We look at each other, dumbfounded that we have been saved and somehow still together after the storm.

"Apart from perched on a beautiful yew tree among the clouds, where are we?" asks Pascal, tucking his shirt into his trousers.

Anil presses her ear to the gnarled tree trunk. "I'm picking up vibrations from this yew tree, from deep down in its roots," she says after a while. "It's one of the oldest trees in Ray Wood."

"You mean that you understand the language of the Wood Wide Web beyond simple vibrations?" I ask in amazement.

"It isn't hard," she replies. "It's all about listening, sensing and concentrating very hard to be able to tune in, a bit like telepathy or radio waves. Give it a try."

I put my ear to the tree trunk, close my eyes and hold my breath to see what sounds I can pick up. I use my thoughts to thank the tree for giving us a place to rest, protected by its needle-like leaves. After a few moments, I sit back stunned. I stare at the group around me. "Anil's right. The yew is happy that we have settled in its branches. This is where Charlie the chaffinch made his wish. The yew is one thousand years old." I press my ear closer to the bark. "Just a minute," I say concentrating hard, "the yew has a cousin in Perthshire that is over two thousand years old!"

At that moment, the butterflies that were ripped out of Anil's headdress in the storm settle back down. "I'm so pleased," she says. "My friends have returned. I was sad at losing them."

"Shhh," says Kobalos. "Listen to the birdsong."

Familiar voices of blackbirds, starlings, chaffinches and lapwings, all wintering in the woodland, drift through the clouds celebrating the end of the storm. Above their chorus, I recognise Robbie's solo. He reports that, without warning, woodlands all over the country were damaged by a terrible storm: trees were uprooted, others had branches snapped off. Foresters have arrived to drag logs away and clear up fallen trees. Thankfully, Robbie tells us, the sheltered guesthouses on Skelf Island have weathered the storm, even those made of straw. But this has not been the case in many woodlands in other parts of the country.

"We should be helping," says Anil. "Our homes at Cabilla are vulnerable, Sky. They may be among those destroyed."

We begin the long climb down the tree through thick clouds without getting very far and are forced to stop as we can hardly see where we are heading.

"Everything happens for a reason," I say, huddling up close to the others.

"You mean, there's a point to the West Wind

bringing us here?" asks Kobalos.

"Exactly," says Anil. "It put us on the branches of a magical tree for a purpose, *and* caused the clouds, making it almost impossible for us to leave. As Sky knows, on the day Robbie brought the invitation, a breeze attempted to wake me up at my home by whispering a warning. I was half asleep and couldn't quite hear. But a moment ago, the same breeze returned and passed right beside my ear. This time, I heard every single word."

"What did it say?" I ask.

"The powerful Four Winds created last night's storm at the temple to show how angry they are about warming temperatures all over the world. They are furious that their power is becoming uncontrollable, increasingly causing destruction. Like us, they too cannot cope with bad air in the atmosphere," replies Anil.

Kobalos nods in agreement. "That was easy enough to understand from their performance last night."

"But there's more to it." Anil lowers her voice to a whisper. "Apparently, the Four Winds got together at the temple and decided they need help. I thought it was part of my dream at the time – the westerly breeze bringing us to the safety of the West Wind, settling on the wings of a falcon-shaped cloud – but we now know that it wasn't a dream at all. The breeze whispered that the Four Winds would like to work with us. They have agreed to calm down if we can help bring about change."

Kobalos's eyebrows rise with curiosity.

"What on earth can *we* do?" I say looking anxiously in his direction. "We have few skills and no experience. That's far too much of a responsibility to be forced upon us," I say in a strained voice.

"It must be why the Four Winds chose to take us by storm on the night before the Nature Summit," suggests Liam.

"I have an idea," Pascal says, perking up. "Lydia, a sprite I met at dinner, would be perfect for joining us and is on a mission to help developing countries use green energy. Her concern is to help places affected by weather disasters. She insists that powerful nations that have benefited from progress through burning coal must join together to take responsibility and put things right."

"Ah," says Kobalos. "Yes. She has the quality of integrity."

Catching hold of this thought, something shifts in my mind. I rigorously clap my hands. "Totally," I say. "I remember you dancing with Lydia last night. She could really help, and is sure to know what we should do."

Anil nods enthusiastically. "I also met an inspirational sprite last night. His name is Anito. He works with a youth group encouraging individuals to make environmentally friendly choices. You'd be amazed by how effective ordinary people can be when they join forces and work for a common purpose."

"Like ants, you mean," I smile.

"Yes," answers Anil. "Successfully working together as a team with shared aims without the need for conflict."

"Together, we will draw a mighty team around us to protect nature all over the world," I say with confidence.

"What about using your magic?" asks Liam.

"Real magic comes when sprites glow together with all the colours of the rainbow and make the same wish," I say. "I'm afraid that Anil and I can't exactly help you yet."

"Maybe you'll find the colour of your true nature earlier than you think," Kobalos says with encouragement.

I smile back at him, feeling a sudden strength within me.

* * *

Waiting for the mist to clear, I overhear Liam and Anil chatting and can't help myself from eavesdropping.

"I meant to ask you, Liam," says Anil, "apart from managing crowds and telling stories, what other kind of work do you do?"

"I cheer people up," he answers, croaking like a frog and making Anil laugh.

"Surely that doesn't count as a job, does it?"

"You'd be surprised," Liam says. "Making other people laugh is quite a skill, I can tell you."

"The oddest things set me off," says Anil. "The work my sister and I do in the wood is so serious that a good laugh lightens our mood and makes us feel connected. Luckily, we both share a quirky sense of humour and are learning to laugh at ourselves."

"The more ridiculous, the funnier," says Liam.

Robbie flies overhead, providing the latest bulletin from the woodland. We all listen.

"Lydia, the conservation warrior," he chirps, "has heard from the Four Winds that guests attending the Nature Summit blown away by the storm have settled safely on the branches of the oldest yew tree in the centre of Ray Wood."

We look at each other pleased to hear the news reported, as otherwise Woodland Welfare Workers would have had to send out a search party to find us.

"Lydia," Robbie continues, "is helping to clear up fallen trees to make way for visitors arriving at the gathering in the temple at eleven o'clock this morning." I fly over to Anil and sit down beside her so that we can listen to the news together. "Many held on by their roots, but some of the younger trees didn't make it. Several of the older ones were seriously damaged." I place an arm around Anil's shoulders to comfort her. "Lydia has salvaged burr walnut and oak for design fairies to carve into wardrobes, tables and chests. Logs have been left for fungi, woodlice, beetle grubs and wood wasps to make into their homes. Damaged old trees have been cut down to the ground to stimulate new growth. These carefully managed coppiced areas will bring sunlight into the woodland, helping new wildflowers to grow and giving a more varied woodland habit for wildlife."

I picture a cricket playing with a grasshopper twice its size in the coppiced fairy glade where we grow our vegetables. Anil turns to look at me and sends a telepathic image she just made up of a grinning tomato.

"Lydia," continues Robbie, "will visit the yew tree in Ray Wood to check that all are safe and sound." In his usual fashion, job done, Robbie bobs his tail and flies off to spread the word further afield.

12

A TEAM

Lydia appears before breakfast, an apparition through the clouds, shining the orderly blue of calm, carrying a picnic basket.

"Hello," I say, getting up, amazed to see her, even though we have been expecting her.

Pascal reaches out his hand in welcome and introduces Lydia to us one at a time.

"I dropped in to see the fairies on Skelf Island on my way over here," she says. "They insisted that I bring you these leftovers to build up your strength before the summit," she says, placing the basket on the fork of the branch beside me.

"Thank you," I say, opening the lid and sharing the pies with everyone. They are warm and wrapped in napkins.

"I was so close to your lodgings," says Lydia, "that I thought you might appreciate a change of clothes and went to fetch them." Lydia passes us a duffel bag containing our face flannel, a hairbrush, toothbrush, leaf pinafore, woollen tights and sweaters. "Charlie will pick up your other things when he collects the picnic basket to take them back to your guesthouse later."

"Perfect," I say, echoed by Anil. We share a thought between us that Lydia is as thoughtful as she is remarkable.

We ask to be excused while we get changed. This we easily achieve engulfed by the cloud on our branch. In the cold light of day, we feel much better to be out of our fancy finery. Anil places our party dresses in the bag and hangs it on a twig beside the picnic basket for Charlie to collect.

All of a sudden, I hear a crackly, rustling sound that I do not recognise.

"Look," shouts Anil. "The wind is bringing us a

beautiful gift."

"No!" cries Lydia to my surprise. "That flying, dancing, shiny object is a crisp packet carried by the wind. It is made from metallised plastic, cannot be recycled, and it is particularly harmful to woodland creatures."

"The Three Ws do their best to keep the woodland clear of all human-made debris that does not belong. It is the first time Anil and I have ever seen such a thing." I say, standing up and wiggling with a playful frown on my face.

Anil flies up on a breeze and catches the crumpled crisp packet. She crinkles it in her hand before bringing it back to the tree. "No doubt another warning from the wind," she says without hiding her delight at catching it before it could blow away.

I take the packet from Anil and fold it small enough to place at the base of the basket for safekeeping. I, too, notice how attractive – and deadly – it must be to unwary creatures. I remember the little mouse nearly choking before sneezing out the small white object. It turned out to be a plastic bottle top identified by the Three Ws. I feel a sense of horror that products such as these are put in the way of innocent creatures going about their daily lives, foraging for food and collecting materials to build their homes.

"Picking up plastic is one of my jobs, so I know all about it," says Lydia floating above us.

"After last night's protest by the Four Winds," I say, "would you help guide us in the right direction to bring climate change under control?"

We all clap to show our united eagerness.

"I'd be delighted to," she says.

A warm current of air passes through, dissipating the cloud and revealing a handsome sprite sitting elegantly in the lotus position on the branch beside us.

Anil waves. "Anito. How long have you been there?"

Glowing the bountiful green of hope, Anito stands up and bows respectfully. "I was hurled up into the sky by the Four Winds during dinner and arrived here at a similar time as you folks," he says. "I have heard your discussions and would be honoured to be part of your team to calm the weather down."

"That's great," we say all at once.

"Networking is key," adds Lydia. "Together, we have the power to educate, changing the way people behave. We can help them refuse practices that go against nature."

"That's the spirit," says Anito. "The world will eventually change for the better if everyone pulls together and refuses to purchase plastic. And it must not stop there. The manufacturing of most things pushes horrible gases into the air. We must try and stop people endlessly buying things they don't really need and find a way for them to shop with the good of everyone else in mind. Think about it."

I do precisely as Anito suggests and conjure up a scene in my mind.

Anil picks this up immediately and talks the others through my thoughts.

"Sky is picturing a family with two children pushing a shopping trolley in a supermarket. To one side of the aisle is a section selling four apples in plastic wrapping. They are all exactly the same as each other and look perfect. On the other aisle, a slightly different variety is set in neat rows, one on top of the other.

"The mother picks a packet of plastic ones, to see what it says on the label.

"'Are they selling four apples for the price of three?' asks the dad, but the mother shakes her head to answer no. 'Actually, I wanted to check that they are local and have not been sent here by air or sea,' she says. 'Local apples always taste so much better.'

"The family pick a loose apple each from the pile under a sign that reads *local produce*. When buying tomatoes and cucumbers in another aisle, the same options are offered. When they come to the section selling crisps, the parents ask their kids to make a choice. Although the metallic plastic bags are pretty, their education tells the children to pick out a plain paper bag instead. These have been dipped in beeswax to keep the crisps fresh.

"At the checkout, the cashier says: 'Congratulations, no plastic. You have ten points awarded to your family footprint for making environmentally friendly purchases. You can save your points and receive a free purchase or have a refund to spend where you please.' The shoppers leave feeling happy that they have contributed to help fight climate change and even have extra money in their pockets."

The image fades from my mind and Anil finishes describing it to the others.

"I like the idea of a footprint," says Liam. "I can imagine thousands of them in wet sand, toes pointing forwards, ready to make a positive path leading towards helping nature."

"I agree," says Lydia, "but we call it a *carbon* footprint. This means that the family Sky has described is reducing the amount of greenhouse gases generated due to their better choices while shopping."

"Ah, and a reason to be rewarded," Anil confirms. "What if the customers can choose to receive a nut, seeds or an acorn instead, to plant in a pot to see if it will grow?"

"Oh yes," says Kobalos. "If any of these grow into saplings, I will ask if I can plant them in a Woodmeadow woodland, where I work as a volunteer planting a wide range of trees, shrubs, wild flowers and herbs that encourage diverse ecosystems to evolve and flourish."

I clap with vigour. It would be wonderful if visitors could enjoy a woodland and watch it grow as they too grow older. "To make it easy for everyone," I say, "families would drop the sapling in a pot at their local nursery, giving their name, ready for the young tree to be collected and planted out in new woodland somewhere local."

"It's a great idea. I'd do it right away," Pascal calls out. "How lovely that everyone would be able to visit their own tree, watch it grow and give it a hug." We pass a smile around with a sense of satisfaction that our idea might work.

We all turn to a creaking sound above us. A woodland sprite glowing indigo purple characterising creativity and resistance to authority descends from a higher branch, rubbing her head.

"Hello," she says a little shakily. "My name is Layla. I think I was knocked out, thrown against a tree trunk by the wind." She sniffs the air to pick up on her bearings. "I don't know what happened or how I got here from the Midlands. I remember a furious storm last night in the woodland where I live," says Layla looking towards me and sitting down.

"What happened?" asks Anil.

"Yesterday morning, the sun came up as usual and shone brightly as the birds began to sing. I came out of my treehouse to hang clothes on the washing line. All of a sudden, a dark cloud descended. Above the birdsong, I heard an altogether different kind of sound. A menacing noise growing louder and louder. The songbirds, sensing danger, flapped their wings and bobbed their tails in warning and flew off into the distance. There was no more singing, no animal or insect anywhere in sight. Whatever they were afraid of, they had left without sticking around to find out. Then, over the brow of the hill, coming down an ancient pathway between hedgerows, a digger loomed like a monster with enormous wheels making thick heavy tracks in the soft ground.

"Diggers had arrived to destroy a section of my woodland," she says hoarsely, looking at each of us in turn. "It will make way for the new train line. They destroyed my treehouse because it was in their way.

"Then last night, no longer with a home, the angry wind took me up with such a force that I called out for help. I imagined that I travelled here on the wings of a giant bird, or so it seemed, like a magic carpet bringing me to safety."

"Same here," says Anil, fluttering her wings in greeting. "That's what happened to us, but you must have come a very long way."

"The destruction was all for a train line that is to be built from London to towns in the north to give commuters a faster journey. Work has begun from London up to Birmingham. It is planned to continue the new railway to Scotland. Over sixty woodlands will be harmed," says Lydia. "Animals camping in Ray Wood are ready to march to the Temple of the Four Winds before the Nature Summit starts in protest for exactly the same reasons Layla has described."

"I'd like to talk to them," I say remembering that Robbie had told me they would be camping out in Ray Wood. "I fear for animal habitats."

"It's not only the devastation," says Pascal joining it,

"but even the woods that remain will have disturbance and harsh sounds generated by trains coming and going."

"You will have a new home soon enough, Layla," says Anito. "But animal territories are another matter."

"I agree," says Liam. "Let's remember what I said last night: where there's a will, there's a way!"

"Totally," says Lydia. "Today is our opportunity to help conservation sprites do something about the threats facing wildlife, nature and the Four Winds."

In the stark light of the early morning, we climb down the yew tree, ready to listen to what the animals have to say.

13

ANIMALS IN PROTEST

Hundreds of animals have grouped beneath the yew tree, making it impossible for those of us without wings to descend to the ground. We hear their howls and barks as we make our way down the tree, including nocturnal animals wide awake when they ought to be fast asleep. The din they're making tells us they're impatient to share their stories and fears about the places they once called home.

Anil and I climb down and settle beside Lydia and Layla on a low branch across from Liam, Pascal and Anito. Lydia flies up and to a central position between us, not too high above the animals so that they can hear her.

"Hello and welcome," says Lydia, hovering above

the huddled crowd. "We appreciate that you have travelled all this way to share your concerns about the new train line destroying your woodland, leaving you without homes, and we are here to listen."

A brown hare with long black-tipped ears bounds forward, tapping a sizeable hind foot aggressively on the chilly ground.

"Then listen carefully and make sure you take note of what I have to say," he begins in a gruff tone. "I ran over three hundred miles from my home in the south these last few days, just to come here and have my say. I am the elected representative for many meadow mammals who could not make it here," he says with an air of importance. "Meadow moles on my patch have lived in their underground tunnels for generations. When the bulldozers began their work, I saw moles and voles run down into their burrows with lightning speed, terrified and confused, searching for safety. The bulldozers blocked the entrances to their tunnels. I don't know if they ever came up again, as our meadow was destroyed, flattened to a mass of mud.

"Now I have nowhere to live," he says banging the

ground. "Brown hares need the shelter of the woodland during the winter. I left my family huddled together beside a tree, traumatised and fearful for their future. Our home has been destroyed and the woodland beside it has been damaged, which is why I am here. I demand action and answers!"

A red fox with a bushy tail pushes through, its ears pricked. "Same here," he says with a growl. "The land has been cleared for the new line right beside my den at Little Lyntus." I nudge Anil sending a message that it was just as well we had made the detour to see the devastation for ourselves. "I don't know what to do. I've been told to move, which makes me anxious. I know every inch of my woodland territory – why should I be forced to move somewhere new? I have come all this way north to ask what we can do to scrap the new train line and restore the devastated areas back as they were before."

"But the damage has been done and can't be undone," says the hare. "We can't ever go back."

"Restoring woodland can happen, but it takes time," replies Lydia with a level voice, hoping to calm the anger in the fox and the hare. "The best we can do is to try and stop the line going further and ruining more habitats."

A hawfinch flies down from a high branch. "My kind are in decline – we have fewer and fewer numbers. I was settled in woodland in the Midlands, but the train will pass right through our wood. We will feel the vibrations in the branches where we would like to nest. With this kind of treatment, I have half a mind to migrate to another country where we can feel safe, never to return."

"It's all very well for you birds," shouts a rabbit. "You migrate here and there, spoilt for choice, with second homes overseas. My family had a lovely burrow in a large warren in a glorious stretch of grassland. We thought we were safe there. Our home is more than three metres deep and has many entrances and exits. But the diggers have filled these with mud. Some of us got out in time and were relocated by Woodland Welfare Workers. Others were taken to new places, far from family and friends. The more docile animals might be happy with that sort of situation, but it's not for me!"

A badger raises his head. "Bulldozers have not

reached my neck of the woods yet, but they will soon come north with their destroying machines. All we ask is the basic freedom to choose where we live in our natural habitats," he says in a deep angry voice.

"I have so many children," says a long-eared rabbit, taking no notice of the badger, "and I will not be welcome to join another warren. Rabbits are protecting their territories, bucks running up and down boundary lines marking their land. I fear for my family. I have left them unprotected and vulnerable. What are you going to do about it?" she yells, looking around her for support.

The crowd of animals respond by growling, shouting and hissing. The noise is tremendous. Animals begin to turn on each other, finding their situation unfair, comparing their circumstances, all speaking at once, baring their teeth, snarling, squawking, flexing their muscles and showing their claws.

Lydia flies towards them, flapping her wings vigorously. "STOP!" she calls, clapping her hands. Taking advantage of their sudden attention. "We're on your side and want to find a solution. Try to see yourselves not as victims, but at the start of new beginnings, ready to live in peace and friendship."

"Good intentions are all very well," says an elderly badger. "But I don't trust other wild animals. They are all out to help themselves, not each other."

I feel like there is absolutely nothing I can do to help them. I put my head in my hands in desperation and wish with all my heart to find a way to some sort of solution. Out of the sky, the West Wind must have heard me. It descends as a falcon-shaped cloud and picks me up. When I open my eyes, I find that the cloud has taken me above the tree. The rest of my team and all the animals are looking up at me in astonishment. I settle on the wings of the falcon, who flies until everyone is out of sight, and keep wishing.

Far away on the horizon, I watch a colourful haze heading towards me. As it draws closer, it becomes clear that this is no haze but sprites. I stand up on tiptoes and wave my arms to attract their attention.

Then it happens. First, there's a humming sound, then a whirring whirlwind above my head grows larger and larger, rotating faster and faster, reaching high up into the Universe. My first fear is that I will be sucked up into it, but soon realise it is quite the opposite. The wind is howling, rotating around and around with something inside it. I look up into the funnel and see the object coming straight towards me. It is a wish travelling at high speed. I catch it with both my hands and only just manage to cling onto it.

This should be my Eureka moment when everything becomes clear. But, preoccupied with the animals and distracted by the approaching sprites, I can't concentrate on the wish and quickly place it in my pocket to look at later.

The sprites draw closer. From the way they are dressed, I can tell that they're urban nature sprites. Their leader, glowing a deep, powerful burgundy, flies in front. Heading for the temple, they see me and make a diversion towards Ray Wood to quickly join me on my cloud.

"Good morning," he says. "My name is Jonathan. I am an Urban Welfare Warrior, and my job is to oversee nature in cities. I have invited urban sprites from all over our United Kingdom to listen at the Nature Summit.

Together, we offer our help in support of displaced animals, insects and birds. We heard they would be protesting and have a solution to offer them."

"I've just caught a wish," I tell him, unable to contain my astonishment that everything seemed to be happening all at once. "It came when I least expected it while I was making a wish of my own. It hasn't made everything clear, though. I feel as though I am in a fog."

"From what I've heard about wishes, you must have really meant yours to have another one sent for you to catch at the same time. Have you read the wish you caught?" he asks.

"No, I put it in my pocket."

"Keep it there until you feel ready to read it. When you do, that's when everything will become clear. I promise."

"Thanks. But, Jonathan, *you* have come to answer the wish I made – it was to help the animals find new homes. They are so agitated. Will you and your team tell them what you can do to help them?"

"Of course," says Jonathan following me down to meet Lydia, Layla and Anito sitting on the branch beside the others. They all look puzzled as urban sprites settle on the branches. I hover above the angry protestors with Jonathan at my side.

"Animals, insects and country folk," I begin. "My name is Sky, and I care so much about you and what has unfairly happened to you and your homes that I made a wish with all my might to do something about it. Jonathan answered my call for help and will tell you what he can do for you."

I return to the branch to sit beside Anil, and Jonathan goes forward to speak.

"Hi there, country creatures great and small. No doubt you are surprised to see urban nature sprites here today in this beautiful woodland setting," he begins. "We have come to help you from towns all over the country." His strong voice attracts animals to group and gather together to listen beneath him. "We met up last night in Birmingham to compare notes about work on the new train line from London. We worry about trains travelling that fast, killing any insect that comes within a whisper of its way. Groups of us have toured the woodlands that have already been affected and seen the devastation to your habitats."

The wilder animals grunt – an affirmation that they have been wronged.

"Our urban cities can provide new habitats for mammals, amphibians, invertebrates and all manner of insects that would like to join us."

"Animals living in the city? That's ridiculous," hoots a bad-tempered owl.

"Many people in cities," Jonathan continues without being put off his stride, "have created ponds in their back gardens and wish to attract pollinating insects and birds to roof gardens on the top of office blocks and high-rise buildings. Terraced houses provide window boxes growing flowers and herbs, and are placed on sills attracting butterflies and bees," says Jonathan pausing to allow the listeners time to share the information, chirping, nattering and buzzing among themselves. Above their chitchat, birds confirm that they like the idea of living on top of a skyscraper, their eggs perfectly protected from ground predators.

"Urban sprites campaigned," he goes on, "and have succeeded in creating valuable habitats in scrubland, planting trees and connecting people with nature. We have already helped transform former garbage dumps into thriving nature reserves."

I can hardly believe my ears and remain in my place with my mouth hanging open.

"That's wonderful to hear," says Lydia.

"My fellow sprites further up the tree have full details to pass onto those of you interested in living in our nature settings in urban areas."

A cheer goes out. The brown hare bangs his hind foot on the ferny floor with approval and even the long-eared rabbit hops about delighted by the idea of starting her own colony.

"There's something else you should know," says Jonathan, looking at the animals. "I am here with my team to campaign for the existing train lines to be improved, instead of building unnecessary new ones, and will send out a news report to you all with the outcome.

"I must leave now," says Jonathan. "My team will remain here to answer all your questions and to put your minds at rest about moving and where will suit you best."

But as soon as Jonathan leaves, the colours in the sky tell us that it is time to make our way to the Nature Summit too.

Those on foot tread a path through the rhododendrons and exotic plants in Ray Wood, while I glide with sprites and fairies over the sodden ground and fallen trees, all making our way together towards the Temple of the Four Winds.

14

THE NATURE SUMMIT

I recognise guests from the party last night piling into the temple. Nature sprites are no longer in their finery but dressed in clothes corresponding to the nature they protect. Our four hosts wearing their Roman robes greet us on behalf of the Four Winds and ask us to take our seats. There are long tables and chairs for speakers, and benches in rows for spectators flanking the four walls.

A talented musician plays an Elven harp. Instead of a folksong, as I would have expected, a fairy with an angelic voice sings the words of a poem written especially for the occasion. I listen carefully. It is about a dream-like state, where rules and natural laws of the old world feel in flux, full of danger and out of kilter, but still not beyond the control of the person who sleeps. The sleeper is full of doubt and distrust but finds enough personal courage to face the future. In so many words, the poet implies that there is still hope to help save the Four Winds from an overheating climate.

The room has taken on a serious mood. Two sea sprites enter through the south door in seaweed robes. Lydia greets them like old friends and introduces them to us as Sam and Dan. Anil and I say hello. Sam tells us he is an ocean sprite and a resident on the Rainbow Warrior boat, presently moored in Liverpool.

Nature sprites from overseas are escorted by helpers and shown to their places alongside conservation speakers. Spectators representing woodlands, oceans, peatlands and meadows gather around the room, ready to listen. Anil and I sit on a bench towards the back, close to the entrance of the West Wind.

"Tell me about the wish you caught," Anil whispers in my ear. "Where and what is it?"

"It's burning a hole in my pocket just waiting to get

out," I say. "But I'm not ready to look at it, not just yet. Not until speakers have told their nature stories."

"Why did the West Wind take you above the tree to catch it? I tuned in to you, but lost the connection."

"I'm not sure, but I have a feeling that everything is about to fall into place."

"But I thought that catching a wish was meant to be a Eureka moment, making everything clear?"

"All I can say is that it's a bit like fog right now – I can see that it's about to clear but must wait for it to lift. First, I have to be sure that I can be relied upon to make the wish come true. According to Jonathan, catching it is just the beginning."

"You can count on me to help you," she smiles.

Robbie sends a tweet to welcome us from a perch set up for birds reporting the event. It is just as well that we have already experienced the impact of this magnificent place at the thanksgiving ceremony. Now we can turn our minds to serious matters.

We spot Pascal sitting with other pixies and Kobalos

is with him too. Anil and I watch Jonathan follow the host for the North Wind to the big square table in the middle to sit next to Lydia.

"I wish we could have stayed at the party longer last night," Anil says, "but arriving in the yew tree and making new friends was such an adventure, wasn't it?"

Unlike yesterday, there is much chattering among sprites and fairy folk, especially discussing the storm and how it had affected them. Sadly, some sprites and a few fairies have lost their homes and have had to make alternative arrangements. We look around to see if there is anyone we recognise from articles we have read in the *Weekly Woodland News*.

"Look!" says Anil, pointing at a sprite glowing emerald green sitting at the long table.

"Who's that?" I ask.

"No less than Miss Scaffold!" she says, dropping her mouth wide open in exaggerated surprise.

"What on earth is she doing here?" I ask with the thrill that I might have a chance of meeting her.

"Perhaps she's one of the speakers," Anil suggests.

"I do hope so," I say. "Life has suddenly become so exciting."

"I know, but ssssh," says Anil, digging me in the ribs.

Titania, Queen of the fairies, flies up to the centre of the dome from her place on her throne. She is as bright and beautiful as a shining star.

"Welcome to our Nature Summit generously hosted by the Four Winds in their glorious temple. Those telling us their stories today have requested that they receive no applause, cheers *or* boos in response to their tales.

"After last night's storm, I spent the morning alone with the Four Winds on the hilltop. They explained that their demonstration was in protest of what feels like a war against nature. They do not wish to cause harm and understand what sprites are up against, with many of you on the front line bearing the brunt, as they do, of the effects of bad gasses in the atmosphere around the world."

A wave of affirmation passes along the benches and

throughout the room. I notice Miss Scaffold raise her hands about to clap, but remembering the request made by Queen Titania, she places them into her lap, looking around her and blushing crimson.

"Nature has always been our teacher," Queen Titania says in a gentle voice. "It has cared for us with kindness, but now the Four Winds have risen up and say they must be cruel in order to get our attention. We can no longer sit here doing nothing, and our focus must now be of prevention. If we all do something, each act of goodness will add up to an enormous sum, greater than any chest of gold. Faery folk the world over supporting nature can rescue the planet and save a threatened future from overwhelming the Four Winds."

Our automatic response is to clap and I am not alone in fluttering my wings instead. I see that Miss Scaffold does it too, so it must be alright. Queen Titania, returns to her throne under the dome.

I look for Liam and as I spot him seated in a far corner, he stands on a high chair to perform his role of introducing the speakers.

Lifting his chin, he sends forth a clear voice. "I call upon snow and ice sprites to tell their stories from Antarctica, Alaska and the North Pole."

Four sprites in thick sweaters and knitted woollen hats hover in front of the podium. "Hello. My name is Gunnar. The ice is melting where I come from on the North Pole," says the first of the two snow sprites. "It used to melt in the summer but now it melts earlier, and the sea levels are rising. My home will soon be under water," says Gunnar. "It is a warning to us all. Penguins, too, are in decline on the west Antarctic Peninsula, one of the most rapidly warming areas on Earth."

"I am Jon, an ice sprite looking out for Polar bears," says the next. "As temperatures rise, less sea ice forms, exposing the coast. The ocean freezes up later and later every year and for a shorter length of time. Polar bears face dwindling sea ice in their Arctic habitat and less food to hunt."

"My name is Helga," says the third sprite. "I too am an ice sprite. Since walruses cannot swim all the time they rely on sea ice that flows over their foraging grounds as safe havens to rest between dives to the seafloor to feed on clams and mussels. These are melting away and making life dangerous for walruses and their calves."

"I am Amak," says the final sprite. "I am concerned for ringed seals. They depend on Arctic sea ice and almost never come onto land. Warming spring temperatures and early melting separates nursing pups from their mothers."

The four sprites look up to the north, south, east and west, then into the eyes of all of us listening. This time, there is no flapping of wings. We watch them return slowly to their seats.

"There is much to think about," says Liam, leaving us with a moment or two for silent thought. "We will now take a short recess for lunch and reconvene afterwards to listen to stories brought by desert sand sprites from the heat of the Middle East."

15

STORIES FROM AROUND THE WORLD

On leaving the temple, we are offered a picnic rug and a little wooden lunchbox carved with a picture of the temple. Remembering the advice given by Miss Bracken, Anil and I take our picnics and split up to circulate with other nature sprites.

Sam from the Rainbow Warrior ship waves to me, so I join and sit with his special guests, members of MAP – Most Affected People. They say hello one at a time and the first tells me he comes from Puerto Rico, which has faced powerful hurricanes. Another from Pakistan where the monsoons cause damage every year, and others from Namibia, Uganda, Mexico and Bangladesh.

"We want climate justice," they say.

"Oh, of course," I reply, not wanting to let on that I do not know what this means. I know that Miss Bracken said not to be afraid to ask questions, and I wouldn't feel so silly and shy if I'd met them before. I have a feeling that the sprite from Namibia's intuition must have picked up on my dilemma as she kindly helps to explain it.

"We need the rest of the world to be involved with the catastrophes we face," she says softly. "It is a crisis for us. We experience destructive weather conditions due to global warming, and it's coming from other countries burning fossil fuels. We don't think it's fair. What is it like where you come from?" she asks.

"It's beautiful and in the south of England. Although I am a woodland sprite, I live on the edge of the wood, and enjoy the river, the meadow and crops growing up the lane at the farm."

"You are fortunate. In Namibia," she tells me, "crops cannot survive the heat and there is much hunger and drought."

I look at the berries, seeds and raisins in my

lunchbox and wonder what it would feel like if there wasn't always something to be found to help myself to eat on trees and growing in the ground and no rainwater to drink.

"We have terrible wildfires, making it difficult for us to breath," says her friend from Mexico. "And most of Mexico is short of water. The once-mighty rivers are drying up and temperatures are rising to deadly levels."

"In Uganda," says another, "families move to bigger cities as they cannot cope with the unstable climate causing devastating landslides. Whole villages collapse, swallowed up into the earth. Landowners strip woodlands of all their trees to plant sugar cane to make profits. Some of the forests that once gave us protection have been cleared."

"It is not only the floods in Bangladesh," says the next. "With the loss of land, young people lose their dreams and hopes along with it. We are forced to leave our things to find a new life, which may be worse, but we have no other choice than to move away."

Budskap, who formed a similar role at the wedding of the two owls, hits the gong he used the night before with a stick, "Please take your seats in the temple; the next speakers are about to begin."

I embrace the spites I have met from overseas and wish them all the luck in the world. Without knowing any of the answers, I tell them that I will be rooting for them. Anil joins me and we make our way up the steps together. She tells me that she had her picnic with Jonathan and the urban sprites and is keen to visit a city soon.

"Jonathan is very pleased to have helped the displaced animals. He told me that most of them have signed up to the urban project and are even excited about the move. He says change can be a good thing," she smiles. "And it's not a bad thing to explore new territory. What a good thing you made that wish just as he was coming towards us, or the story might have been very different."

"I know. The animals were so angry, and rightly so. Now we have to face the anger over climate justice. It is a very serious topic."

"What does it mean?"

"It means what it says, but I'm only just beginning to grasp what lies behind it and intend to try and do something to help."

* * *

"Welcome, welcome," says Liam once everyone has settled. "We have more first-hand stories to be told, and, as before, to save time, we have decided these will take place one after another without interruption, with a short pause for thought after each." He nods toward a bench where many sprites from overseas are sitting in a long row.

"Following on from the stories about melting ice," says Liam, "I welcome four desert sand sprites who wish to raise alarm bells with a call to action."

The sprites dressed in sandy coloured linen robes make a circle around the dome above Queen Titania's throne, facing onlookers in four directions.

"Good afternoon," says the first. "Temperatures are reaching fifty degrees centigrade where I come from in Kuwait. This is the hottest I've ever experienced. The scorching heat means that I cannot go out most of the day. More and more of the land is drying out and becoming desert, causing temperatures to rise further."

143

"A few years ago," says the next. "I planted trees on a patch of desert near a motorway in Kuwait. Many said it was impossible to plant anything in the sand because temperatures were too high. I had to bring water in tanks, but my trees proved that it can be done."

"Trees provide shade that bring down the temperature by many degrees as well as clean up the air," says the third sprite. "And on top of all that, trees fend off dust and pollution. Hedgehogs and spiny-tailed lizards now visit this oasis to find fresh water and shade. It's a beautiful thing."

"I am calling on you," says the tree planter, "to help us make a large-scale green belt in the desert sand. I have shown that the desert can be planted. We can work together to plant trees and bring temperatures down for the benefit of all."

"It is now too hot for many of us to live and work," says the fourth among them. "I am not from the Middle East, but from West Africa where the heat has grown and grown and is now like fire. My village is close to the edge of the Sahara Desert and I am unable to bear the high temperatures," he says, looking around at his audience. "In the summer, I have become nocturnal and sleep during the day and work during night. Many animals have lost their habitat. They have little water to drink and increasingly less to eat. We cannot survive such extreme heat."

I wanted to clap his courage for speaking up. Instead, I watched each of them return to sit on a bench together in silence.

Next, Sam and Dan, from the Rainbow Warrior ship, stand up. "We're ocean sprites from New Zealand," Sam says. "Did you know that one in three dead turtles that wash up on New Zealand shores have eaten plastic? Turtles eat it, mistaking plastic for jellyfish. The common plastic bag is a deadly killer and the ocean is under threat. Plastic is a master of disguise."

"Plastic lasts for 20 years at sea," Dan says. "It breaks down into micro plastic that never actually disappears."

"Plastic is something we can do something about immediately," adds Sam. "We can stop buying it. Supermarkets and shops can stop selling it. Join us in our campaign to help put a stop to killing marine life."

The Four Winds waft around their temple. From the sounds they make, they tell me that it is time to look at the wish that is sitting in my pocket. Without a second thought, I fly up under the dome, deciding to open it right there and then in front of everyone.

16

EUREKA!

"Excuse me, excuse me, excuse me, everyone for flying up unannounced," I begin. "And, of course, Queen Titania," I curtsey and follow with a bow.

I look down and see hundreds of astonished eyes and quite a few mouths open wide, yet the Winds are right beside me.

"We have heard stories from sprites asking us for our help. I am certain that I will not be alone when I say that I cannot stand by and do nothing when I know that the sprite next to me is in distress.

"We are one world and must learn to be fair and take responsibility for climate justice. This means helping those who are suffering from the worst impacts. Nature sprites are one big family protecting living creatures under the care of nature. We must never let nature down, and we must help the Four Winds by striving for clean air and water for all." Nobody moves. The West Wind gives me a gentle nudge to tell me that it is time.

"Before arriving at the summit this morning," I say, "I caught a wish sent down to Earth by the Four Winds and kept it in my pocket. As we all know, catching a wish makes everything clear. Look," I say pulling the wish out of my pocket for everyone to see. "Here it is! Let's see if we can see things clearly together."

The wish shines the colours of the rainbow with a white light in the centre. "Oh my," I say. "The wish was sent by nature sprites living in and around my home in Cabilla. It has their signature." I pause to look at the wish more closely.

"Eureka!" I shout. "Eureka!' I say again. And suddenly everything becomes clear as crystal.

"The wish asks nature sprites all over the world to work together to calm the weather. We have a shared problem that must be dealt with as a joint effort. The wish says that the only way to make it work is to use our love of competition and strive to do better. They ask me to call sprites to make rainbows connecting continents, islands, seas, rivers, lakes, all as one voice, making one wish, altogether so that this wish I have caught may come true.

"Fairy dust will fall from the rainbows we make, sprinkled like seeds of hope for fairy folk, godchildren and nature sprites to catch hold of to help us achieve the hopes, dreams and aims of the wish I am holding in my hand." I pause for a moment then feel purpose deep within me. "I am ready to do whatever it takes to help the Four Winds settle back to temperatures that are sustainable and bring them calm!"

Everyone claps. Some stamp their feet. On top of all this fanfare, Liam whistles! I cannot believe it and shake my head and flap my arms and wings in protest.

"No, no," I say. "We are not allowed to clap! My words are insignificant compared to what we have heard today." Even so, I see Kobalos jump up and down enthusiastically clapping his hands above his head!

"Please," I say waving my arms, "I don't want praise, I only want your help and support." I can't stop them and the noise gets louder and louder.

To my amazement, Miss Scaffold flies up from her safe seat and whispers in my ear.

"What?" I say. I clasp my hands together and look at my aura. I have a yellow aura the colour of honeycomb, mixed with sunshine. Miss Scaffold confirms that my true nature is of optimism, enlightenment and creativity. I can't help it, I clap for joy and do a cartwheel. I have found my true nature. This really is my Eureka moment. I'm suddenly speechless. Fortunately, Miss Scaffold comes to my rescue.

"My name is Marjorie Scaffold and those of you who are not sprites won't know that I teach nature sprites how to make rainbows all over our country. Sprites I have taught might know that I have been ill for some months due to foul air, with a backlog of sprites to train, resulting in fewer rainbows," she says. "I am overwhelmed by the stories told by nature sprites experiencing catastrophic conditions overseas.

"I am equally impressed by Sky's youthful

enthusiasm, and for finding her true colour to shine. At dawn, I will take Sky by the hand and, with the permission of the Four Winds, call upon the world's sprites to make the rainbows that Sky has described. Together, we will make the unifying wish to catch a shooting star and send it out to the Universe."

* * *

It took quite a time to leave the temple with so much to talk about with the other guests and conservation sprites. In the end, the Four Winds had to give us a gentle push of encouragement, as it was time to draw things to a close and for everyone to leave. Right away, we sent a message to the Three Ws to report on the Nature Summit and, of course, on my news too.

"That was amazing! Your speech, I mean," says Anil. "And opening the wish in front of us all. It was so funny when you didn't know we were all clapping because of your aura glow," she laughed as we giggled our way back to our lodgings.

Anil is overjoyed on my behalf. She's generous, not jealous as I might have been had it been the other way around. But I am sure that it will be her turn to shine before too long. She has a multitude of ideas, is tuned to nature and, on top of it all, she doesn't mind one way or another about finding her own colour to shine.

It is comforting to return to our rooms at the guesthouse on Skelf Island, having only left it the evening before and with so much happening in between. We wash and change into our nightclothes and have a hot cup of soup. Anil admits that she is far too excited to sleep, and the same goes for me. Miss Scaffold will collect me at dawn and I'll have my very first rainbow shower. And we will send our wish to the world to remember how to listen to nature.

Lying in bed, I leave the curtains wide open so that the moon can shine in and onto my face. I am taken to faraway places, eventually fall fast asleep and have happy dreams. The fear of the unknown is rapidly turning into thoughts of adventure and hope for the future of the Four Winds.

THE END

SPRITE SPEAK:

Legitimate = something genuine and worthy

Ruthful = being kind and telling the truth,

the opposite of ruthless

Staccato = A quick thought message,

as precise as musical notes.

Worthy = Having high ideals

Class = Spectacular

CREDITS:

Jonathan, leader of the urban sprites:

Jonathan Dent,

Natural Habitats Manager,

St Nicks Nature Reserve & Environment Centre,

York YO10 3FW

Nature Summit Song

To words by The Poet Laureate,

Simon Armitage:

From his article, *The Guardian*

Fri 5 Nov 2021

using his explanation of his COP26 poem.

ABOUT THE AUTHOR

In 2020, Fleur shifted her focus from an influential career promoting British interior design to writing children's books. Faced with viruses and climate change, Fleur's books look at the magic hidden in nature to understand its delicacies and power to control our lives. Written for middle-grade readers, Fleur weaves stories to help children grow up with a love of nature and potential to protect it.

Photo credit: Andreas Von Einsiedel

BOOK TWO: THE JOURNEY

If you would like me to be in touch about when Book Two is available, please send an email addressed to fleurrossdale@gmail.com

fleur@fleurrossdale.com

Printed in Great Britain
by Amazon